Gold Leaves from Havana

Clare L Rolfe

Rolfe, Clare L.

Gold Leaves from Havana / by Clare L Rolfe

Paperback ISBN 978-0-6450880-5-2

eBook ISBN 978-0-6450880-6-9

Printed and distributed by Ingram Spark

A catalogue record for this
book is available from the
National Library of Australia

Contents

Introduction

This series of stories were inspired by a brief trip to Cuba post Castro. It was a fusion of the heart and mind: sensual and thought-provoking equally. The enduring impressions include the vim and bustle of the people, equatorial heat, and the almost cubist aesthetic of Spanish Colonialism, 1950's American cars interspersed with the heroes of the communist revolution in particular that of Che Guevara.

The history of Cuba prior to and subsequent to the revolution is available for anyone who is interested to inform themselves. Pervading the tour conversations were the polemics around Cuba and the USA.

These stories are not intended to be a critique of the political or economic systems of these countries even though one could write in biblical proportions on those topics. The contrast between each nation in their subordination of the essentials of human need: food, housing, healthcare, and education to political idealism versus wealth creation, form the foundations of how these nations define themselves. One tolerates dissent up to a point while the other retains strict control over information and freedom of speech. Both have used revolutions to achieve independent nation states. Both countries instill a strong sense of national pride and loyalty in their populations.

When reading the protagonists and antagonists about Cuba, both acknowledge the successes of the revolution in terms of removal of a corrupt government, the old *Latifundia system and exploitation from unequal trade agreements with the US. And most importantly improving the education level and healthcare for poorer Cubans.

But its critics speak of the restriction on information and right to express disagreement with the government and its punitive measures to control anything deemed counter revolutionary.

The people themselves have endured significant economic hardship in terms of food and fuel shortages at various times, depending on the mood of the superpowers which have an existential influence in all our lives. And then there are those who fled due to being accused of being anti-government and forced into exile.

It wasn't lost on any of us tourists what it would have been like to work in a sugar cane field all day in forty degrees and mercurial humidity for little or no pay.

When the stories crystallised enough to be begin writing, the old Hollywood Westerns formed the stage setting. These movies developed the popular cultural icons of American Libertarianism. The films were almost dystopian realities where it was the individual surviving in a hostile world with less than noble motivations. This imagery was contrasted against the socialist ideology of Cuba and where that may fit in a future world; a world where AI has constant access to data and information. And like the old westerns there is the ubiquitous Sheriff and the lure of a bag of gold.

Clare L Rolfe

* Latifundia - During the modern colonial period, the Portuguese and Spanish monarchs often rewarded military service with extensive land grants in Brazil, Bolivia, Mexico, Venezuela, Uruguay, Cuba, Chile, and Argentina. The economics depended on slave labour often by the forced recruitment of local labourers and peasants allowed by colonial law.

Hearts of Gold

The sign Bone Town stood above her. It was draped in copper wires and microchips burnished to a perfect glean. The sign dazzled with reflections of sunlight as the breeze drifted over the decorations. Underneath painted in red letters she read "Festivales Satellite Day 1 to now".

The train hissed once more signalling its' shut down. Anne collected her pack and put her mask over her face.

She walked into the main street. A child strode past her talking to a robot constructed from three satellite antennae welded together. They wore matching sombreros made from the dishes. The locals stared at her as she made her way down the street. She was dressed in city attire. The green satin suit with culottes had been her favourite. It gave her confidence and reminded her of a younger self. She walked toward the hotel, inside her heart thudded like a massive drum embedded in her chest. She desperately wanted to turn and get on the train but knew there was no going back. She had walked out on her life after the debtors had come to seek revenge on Jack. She was here because of him, and he was going to make amends to her.

The hotel was nameless. It was three storeys high. The remnants of industrial paraphernalia shaped into a perfect cube matched the rest of the architecture along the street. A clerk looked at her as she walked in.

"Welcome to Bone Town."

"Hello, I need a room for a few nights. Preferably up on the top floor. I like quiet and security."

"Sure Ma'am. We have only one room left on that floor."

"That is fine. Is there a window?"

"Yes, it looks over to the south."

"Ok how much?"

"Well with the festivities and all, it'll be one hundred a night and extra for any juice to plug into the main networks."

"That's a lot. I won't need extra juice. How about ninety a night."

"One hundred or leave it" replied the clerk.

Anne took out the credit chip and handed it over. The clerk swiped it.

"Just follow the stairs to the top and you will see the room directly ahead" spoke the clerk as he placed a bracelet on her wrist.

Anne puffed slightly as she reached the top of the stairs. She swiped her bracelet to open the room. Inside was a single bed, on the opposite wall a window with a writing desk butted up against the sill. At the end of the room, was the bathroom. The entire space would have been no than one metre by two metres.

She put her backpack on the desk and looked out the window. Across the boundary wall, she saw the sweeping Arizona desert. It was rocky interspersed with massive cacti. Irradiated by the collapse one hundred years ago they thrived and now stood as tall as sequoia pines. Beyond the forest in the shimmering haze, she saw the direction she needed to go.

She took off her coat off and washed in the small basin. The water was refreshing as it removed the fine scum of dust off her skin. She lay down.

She thought of Jack. Her heart swelled with love and anger. She shut out Lucy's face as it beamed back at her.

Jack had told her about this place on his death bed.

"The gold is on the last carriage of the Arizona express. It was meant for you and the girl. Enough to buy your way out of any life associated with me."

"It's stolen Jack" she had replied. "You killed all those people to get a bit of gold. They were honest folk. They didn't deserve to die. No amount would ever make me sleep well knowing that it was bought with the blood of honest folk. If I ever get that gold, then I will return it to whoever owns it. Tell me where it comes from so, I can make amends."

"They stole it from the backs of their labourers and then the bank stole it from them. No one is innocent of a crime here."

"But the bank didn't steal it with their lives."

He had grunted at her innocent comment "What about the people who perished in the fields or children who didn't have enough to eat to keep the wealthy ones overfed?"

Anne didn't answer him. She had followed his eyes as he had looked across at Lucy.

"She will be fine. I'll get her educated. That will be her wealth."

"They'll come after you. The gold is the best chance to escape and buy your freedom."

"I know but you brought them here in the first place. Is that what this was all about Jack. Freedom."

"What else is there?" he had replied

"Us. There was us. You are a fool. You doomed us to be criminals."

"Go to the fall zone. It's dangerous but if you're quick, you'll be ok. I stayed too long, and the poisoned air got into me."

Those were his last words to her as she had sat dutifully beside him watching him take his last breath.

So now she lay with greed in her heart and blood on her hands. Lucy was stashed away in one of the colleges in San Fran. Hopefully she would forget about her mother and remain anonymous to the debt collectors.

She rubbed the scar on her stomach where the prod of the debtor had struck her. She had managed to wrestle it away from her and land a lethal blow as well. She shuddered at the memory of all the blood that had burst out of the woman's body.

She clenched her hands in anger again "It was your fault Jack."

The firecracker screaming through the air startled her out of her musing. Looking out of the window toward the street below, the smoke of the exploding crackers cast a pale blue haze. She saw the motheaten moon through the cacophony of burning mineral powder.

"You look as worn out as the world" she said to the forlorn moon. Colonised and mined so now great pock marks dotted its once sacrosanct face.

Her stomach rumbled. The sound of a piano and clapping echoed through the windowpane, signalling the saloon down the street was in full swing.

She put her suit on and tidied her hair. The air didn't catch in her throat here, so she left her mask behind.

The clerk watched her as she walked out. She heard the noise of a crowd cheering. Another firecracker went off. It was up toward the train station.

Walking into the bar she saw a group of men sitting together. They were playing cards. A few more people were scattered around.

"Ma'am, spoke the bartender."

"I'm looking for a meal, and some absinthe."

Turning he grabbed a fluorescent green bottle and a glass.

"Tonight's special is fake steak and soup. If you are still hungry there is even some cactus pie for sweets."

"Sounds delicious, how much?"

"On the house tonight ma'am, being the first day of the festivals."

Anne took the glass and toasted the bar tender.

"I was wondering who I would talk to about hiring labourers for some work I need to do?"

The bartender looked furtively over her shoulder.

"You'll have speak to the Sheriff. He's only one who grants license for any paid work. He is over there. The one with the big black hat.'

She saw the man he was talking about. His face was hidden by a large black hat. A smoking cigar poked from underneath the rim. Its end went red suddenly as the lawman sucked in a breath. No smoke was expired out she noticed. It was like he ate it.

"Thankyou."

She hadn't planned on needing to go through the law. She had money to offer any mercenary to help her. It was risky but it was too risky to use a sheriff. They would know it was stolen goods.

As she had turned to sit at a table, she noticed one of the men playing poker beside her at the bar. He tipped his hat to her. She nodded and went to sit down.

The steak was good. She hadn't eaten this well in many years. She had scrimped and saved to make the journey and have enough to pay for help to finish the job.

"Ma'am"

She looked up as she put the last piece of steak in her mouth.

She chewed slowly as she acknowledged the man before her. His face was still cast in shadow and the light from the ceiling darkened it even more. She looked at his elegant hands. Rings encased very finger. Gold rings two and three on each digit glinted in the dim light.

She took a sip of absinthe.

"Sheriff. The food is very good here."

"Yes, it is ma'am. The bartender said you had some work needed to be done?"

Anne looked at the bartender he avoided her gaze. Her plans were destroyed in that moment. There was no choice now, she would have to rely on the law to help her.

"Yes sir, I do. He mentioned I will need to speak to you."

"Yes. If you come in the morning, we can talk about what needs to be done."

"Yes, thankyou Sheriff. Will ten be fine?"

"Yes, ma'am it will. Over at the courthouse. The bartender will tell you where it is."

He left. She swallowed the last gulp of food. Her heart thudded. His eyes had flickered briefly in the light, and they had condemned her to death as a murderer.

"Another?"

She looked up and saw one of the men from the table playing poker. She stared into his brown eyes and instead of a noose she saw an opportunity.

"Thanks. Absinthe, straight."

He came back with a beer and glass and sat down.

"So what work are you offering?"

She eyed him. He had seemed younger than her but not by much. Could he be trusted?

"I think I have to speak to the Sheriff before I do anything else?"

"Perhaps. Not all work needs to go through him."

"I will speak to him in the morning."

He nodded and sipped more beer.

"What sort of man is the Sheriff?" she asked finally.

"Didn't you see his eyes." He put the empty beer bottle down and tipped his hat. "I can be found at the southern end of town. Ask for Juan."

When she left, she saw Juan's shadow walking up the main street. She turned towards the hotel.

Back in her room she lay down. Her head was spinning from the absinthe. The eyes of the Sheriff chilled her again as the green liquor made them appear directly above her on the ceiling of the room. She saw the dots of the surveillance cams forming the dark iris of the eyes. She was surprised that they sold absinthe here. She had become addicted to it once she knew it fried the data signals used to capture any abnormal brain synapses, like violent homicidal urges or subterfuge. She dozed off forcing her mind blank in case her dreams betrayed her.

The morning sun was brighter and rose earlier here than in San Fran. Dawn didn't break much before eleven back home. She checked her scanner band. It was only nine o'clock. She washed and dressed. Her stomach wanted to hurl. She swigged some water in her mouth and swallowed. Her stomach churned but accepted the liquid.

The street was quiet. She saw a woman cooking some quesadilla pockets. There was a robot coffee pot walking toward her with a cup of hot brew. She took it and smiled. She gave the woman a coin for two doughy slices. Sitting on a step next to the woman she drank and ate breakfast. The robot waited patiently to see if she wanted more. She graciously accepted. The coffee was good.

"So ma'am where are you from?" asked the Sheriff.

"I come from Chicago City. I am a widow. My husband was a prospector in the day before satellites were banned and he made a small fortune from the sales of the detritus. That was before the big crash. Any way some of this fortune I have since found out was stolen from other prospectors. I know this because he told me on his death bed. But also, I met by chance one of the wives of those he done wrong. It was when I was working the slums and came across her in the laundries. Her husband had hit the bottle after my husband had stolen his stake. I need to make it right for my daughter and those people. He told me where the rest of that treasure is, and I intend to find it and clear our name so my daughter can be in decent company and make amends to those people wronged."

"Where is this treasure?"

"It is in the desert to the south in a train wreck. I need a guide to take me there and protection against bandits."

"How much are you willing to pay?"

"I will give twenty percent of the spoils to whoever gets me back to the city here and safely on a train to Chicago."

"Seems fair but there is one problem. The desert south is forbidden land and how do I know that what you say is the truth. How do I know you aren't a thief like your husband?"

"You don't Sheriff. Why is it forbidden?"

"It just is. It is not safe and there is nothing there anyway. I think your husband may have been lying. Usually comes along with thieving. He may have been trying to honey a guilty heart."

"True but one thing I know about my Jack he knew where every penny he ever had in his possession lay. He wouldn't have told me if it wasn't real. I need to make justice for these people and make a good name for my Lucy. That must mean something to a sheriff; justice."

The Sheriff broke into a laugh. "Do you mean real or perceived justice ma'am?"

The light from the window hit his face which had been shrouded. He was pale almost translucent.

"Justice means nothing in the face of the law. Laws exist to judge if the justice and truth mean anything real. The wrongs been done by your husband, no recompense is going to make up for the hardship those people endured ma'am. It's about you sleeping easy at night and looking good in front of the so-called decent folk. My justice here is to stop law breaking. That's the best justice I can give. Your request is denied. There is a train back to Chicago tomorrow. Be on it."

She sat there stunned. Five years in the planning and now at the eleventh hour it was all shot to pieces.

"I am speechless sir at your pigheadedness. Not to see the sense of this and the profit for all involved. How else will the world find belief again in good deeds and honest hearts if people cannot make amends for their mistakes. You have no charity in you sir and are less than that badge's meaning."

"It's a grand speech ma'am but I am not here to restore faith in humanity. I am here to stop humanity believing it can do anything it damn well pleases. The human heart never changes, it writes its own rules and justifies them with equal amounts of absurdity and atrocities. There is no lack in its arrogance."

Anne looked defiantly at the Sheriff. Anger swelled at the truth of some of his words, but the resolve to finish what she started sat like a steel rod inside her. As if he had read her mind the Sheriff spoke

"Don't bother trying to make your own way south either. This place is locked down at night. The iron gates are shut and will only be open again to let the train leave."

She got up. She was numb. What did he mean there was no way of leaving until the train arrived?

The Sheriff turned his chair around. She watched the silhouetted figure sitting still as he lit a cigar. Her plans were like those fine fingers of vapour getting sucked inside him. Again, the red tip flared as he inhaled and again like her plans, he feasted on the nicotine, poisoned and clean air alike with no way of escape.

"Enjoy the markets and festivities ma'am. You were lucky you arrived when Bone Town is happy. It isn't usually this way. Deputy show the lady out."

She followed the gaunt youth who looked like the years of working with the sheriff had raped him. She wanted to ask when the first time it had happened to him.

She sat back in the saloon watching a band and a group of children dressed as satellite dishes perform a play about how all the machines crashed to earth and the Sheriffs saved the day. Suddenly a glass and bottle landed on the table in front of her. It was Juan.

"So how did you go?"

"Do you want a job? It will be worth a gold bullion." She replied as she skulled the glass of absinthe.

"What is it?"

"One hundred miles into the Arizona fall zone. Payment is when I am on safe land, away from the north."

Juan had drummed his fingers on the table.

"You know we can't leave before the gates are open. There is surveillance with a thirty-mile radius which are tripped even by a rattlesnake's tail. He will know."

"How then?"

"The train; you will need to jump, and we can backtrack."

"Are you sure? Wont he know you are gone?"

"He will but you don't know how many times he hasn't got me yet."

"Wouldn't he just kill you when you got back?"

"Don't you understand him. It's not about justice or revenge it's about proving the law and if it's been broken. He is no religious zealot or vengeful tyrant. The sheriff only knows one thing the law and unless he can witness it being broken then it ain't broke."

"So where do I jump?"

"You will see a greenstick tree. It's just outside the radar perimeter. Count to thirty and jump. The ground is soft there. I will be waiting."

He slid a napkin across the table toward her. She took it casually as he got up and left. Folded inside was a key card.

The hissing vapour from the train's fusion engine slowly enveloped the black hat of the Sheriff as it drew away from Bone Town. Anne was certain that would not be the last time she would see him. He knew she thought. Somehow, he knew.

She tucked her trousers into her boots and made sure she sat near the door of the carriage facing toward the north. She kept her eyes peeled for the tree. The empty plains of the desert made spotting things easy.

After an hour, a splash of vibrant green appeared. She placed her pack on her shoulder and went out into the standing section of the carriage. She tested the door it was locked. She pulled out the key card Juan had given her. She stood looking through the window of the door. Closer and closer the tree came until it flashed past her.

"1 2 3 4 5 6 7 8 9 10 11 12 13 14 15 16 17 18 19 20 21 22 23 24 25 26 27 28 29 30."

Anne swiped the door latch. Pulled it open and jumped without thinking. She felt a brief euphoria at the feeling of falling but blackout as her body hit the sand. She rolled over confused at her position. Dirt was in her mouth. She lay still, breathing deeply to silence the pain of the impact. She opened her eyes. Nothing just dull aqua sky. She moved. It hurt but it was ok. She sat up and quickly scanned around her. The train had disappeared, and it was only the grassy outcrops among sand dunes which surrounded her.

She saw Juan walking toward her.

"The ground isn't that soft." She scolded as he neared.

He smiled. "It has been a long time." She wondered how he got out of the city.

Juan pulled her to her feet.

"Ok which way?" he asked.

She looked around her. "We need to head west and then directly south. It's below the forest."

He nodded and began walking. She followed limping.

"How long do you think?" she asked.

"I have no idea. This is your treasure hunt" Juan replied.

"How far ahead of the sheriff are we?" Anne asked.

"The train stops at Satellite City. They count the people on and off. They will know they are one short. He will know who it is when they tell him. So maybe a day behind us. He will be on horse so maybe half a day."

Anne's heart sank. It wouldn't be enough time.

"Don't worry. I know a way through this place which will be shorter. He can't bring his horse through the forest and the radiation fields will screw him. He will need to go the long way round." Juan spoke seeing the hollow look of despair on Anne's face.

As dusk seeped into the desert, the cacti forest loomed before them. They entered the silent and imposing succulents. Anne looked up in the dim light and saw that some of the plants were so tall she couldn't see where they finished.

"We will need to wait till light. If we stumble and get jabbed by one of those monsters, it will kill us" spoke Juan.

Suddenly Anne felt tired and needed to lie down. She rolled her pack up and placed her coat over her legs. She watched Juan sit against a rock. He lit a smoke.

"Do you want one?" he offered.

"No thank you. Absinthe's my thing. How long have you lived in Bone Town?"

"I was born there."

"So, your family are there as well?"

"Yes no one leaves Bone Town unless you die."

"Why is that?"

"It's the law."

"But visitors can come and leave?"

"Yes."

"But aren't you curious as to what else is out there?"

"Hmm, sometimes. But the visitors we get are always in a hurry to get away from where they come from, so I guess we just think, it's no better than Bone Town."

Anne conceded Bone Town was the last stop on a train line that went nowhere. And mostly people were trying to get away from something in the north, either the unending cold weather or the debt collectors. Life had become too expensive to live there and everyday revolved around a perpetual fight to pay debt down.

"Yes, but don't you get sick of looking at the same thing every day?"

"Doesn't everyone. Besides we have food, a place to live. We know where we come from."

"Juan why did you help me? I mean why risk your life for money which you are only going to spend in Bone Town?"

"It's how you pay the Sheriff. It's how you live there. Besides I never said I wanted to die in Bone Town. But if I leave, I want to make sure my family can pay the fine to the Sheriff if I escape. Also, I know that it costs a lot to live where you come from. If I leave, I can't come back, and I still want a roof to sleep under. You know in case more satellites fall out of the sky" he laughed as he spoke.

Anne smiled as well. She rolled over and fell asleep.

She woke. She felt the warm flesh of a hand on her face and hot breath in her ear. She struggled.

"Shoo, the Sheriff is riding past. He hasn't seen us." Juan whispered. His lips tickled her ear.

They waited. Just faintly she could hear sand grains being crushed as the horse strode past slowly. It eventually faded. The deep shadow of night had passed, but the stars were still visible in the pre-dawn pallor.

Juan sat back not moving. Anne rolled over toward him.

"That was too close. He will catch us" she whispered.

"No there is still a chance. He needs to go all the way round. It is a three-day journey. For us it should only take a day and night."

"Why can't he come this way?"

Juan looked at her surprised at her question.

"The cactus, they have their own magnetic fields. With all the gold he wears, it would weigh him down."

Anne still didn't get it.

"Why does he wear so much jewellery?"

"Come enough questions. We need to hurry."

"Juan I would have died without you."

"I know." He smiled at her and quickly kissed her on the mouth.

His warmth was enticing. She hadn't been with anyone since Jack and even then, there was no love; just two bodies wanting to eat something else besides food.

They continued picking their way through the forest as the daylight brightened. The heat was palpable from the emissions of the plants. Anne could feel small vibrations on her face and hands where her skin was exposed. She wondered if it would kill her.

"It is dangerous here like the poisoned areas of the desert."

"No, the plants have protective factor against radiation. But their juice would kill you."

"So how can you eat the cactus then?" she asked remembering the slice of pie she had at the saloon.

"There is one part of the plant which is edible and very nutritious It's dangerous work, I lost my brother to that work. I remember the day the Sheriff had ordered everyone out into the forest to harvest the hearts of these plants. It was all because a plague was expected from the north, and the Sheriff wanted everyone protected from the contagion. But only a few of us knew how to cut the plants without being stabbed by their spines. Marco was young, too young. Do you know the hardest part of living in Bone Town Anne?"

"Besides the Sheriff, being locked in an iron fortress every night and not being allowed to leave, no I don't know what the hardest part is Juan?"

"Not being able to speak about my brother's death. It is forbidden to challenge the law when the law has not been broken. My mother wept in silence because, Marco had died doing something legal but unjust. We weren't allowed to express how angry we felt. I want to leave because of that. With gold in my pocket, I can find somewhere I can cry about my brother."

"You know injustice is everywhere Juan?" Anne replied

'Yes, but if I stay my anger will get me killed, and it would mean my mother would have nothing left at all."

"Why don't you take your mother with you?"

"I will one day but she is stronger than me, and she told me to go first to find a way. She said she will last longer than I would, so I needed to leave first."

Anne's heart swelled with pity for Juan. Why she wondered, she had after all had her own injustices like many others in a world now patched back together by the very technology which had half destroyed it.

They stopped around mid-afternoon. Anne collapsed to the ground exhausted.

"I don't know what's wrong with me. I have plenty of water and food."

"Have you had implants put in when you were chipped?"

"Yes probably."

" It would be that weighing you down."

Juan sat down next to her.

"It will be dangerous once we leave the forest. He will sense us. So, we need to be quick ok."

"Yes, I understand. I am only here because of my husband. He left us at the mercy of the debt collectors. I need to get enough to let my daughter remain in college, and so I can live somewhere else. He was a thief and a liar. He killed and cheated people with money scams. I hated him when he died."

"No, you didn't. You are doing this because you still love him. Otherwise, you would have walked away."

"No, you don't understand. He left debts, and the debt collectors are ruthless. They are like the Sheriff. No one ever clears their debts."

"So, you are seeking justice for what your husband did to you and your daughter. You think he owed you something."

"I guess so."

"So, you still love him. And you are hurt he did not love you back in the way you wanted."

"What makes you an expert on matters of the heart?" Anne retorted half irritated he was probably right.

Juan smiled and took her hand.

"It is good to know the human heart is the same wherever it comes from" he kissed her hand.

She didn't pull away.

"Mine is full is greed now. I am sick of owing other people. I don't think I even want to make sure Lucy is ok anymore. I can't change the world for her, she needs to learn to live in it like I had to." Anne felt tears well up, but she choked them back.

Juan looked at her but didn't offer any sympathy.

"Are you ok to keep going? I want to reach the edge of the forest by nightfall and then head into the desert during the night."

"Yes, I think so."

The forest suddenly stopped in a straight line on the edge of a gravel ridge. Juan stepped down and instantly the rocks gave way. He tumbled over and landed against a cactus towards the bottom.

Anne heard him groan with pain. She half slid and ran down to him.

"Juan" she grabbed him and pulled him free. She saw the spines of the cactus in his thigh.

"Oh no."

"Quickly pull them out" he wheezed.

She put her gloves on and pulled the heads of spines out of his leg.

"Oh Juan, it's too deep. I don't have anything to stop the poison seeping in."

"Use the whiskey in my pack." She pulled the bottle out and opened it. She splashed the whiskey directly into each wound. Juan groaned viscerally as the alcohol bit into his flesh. He took the bottle and swigged it.

Anne tore some strips off her shawl and wrapped his thigh.

"Can you walk?" she asked.

Juan got up grimacing. Anne held him as they began to descend into the desert.

"We need to head south now. Directly south. It should only be sixty miles from here" she spoke.

They limped across the dunes together. Anne steadied Juan but by dawn, the poison had begun to take its toll. They sat down together. Juan leant on Anne for support. She held the water cask to his mouth.

"I cannot make it. The fire of the cactus' blood is inside me. I will not make it."

"Oh Juan, it is my fault. You wouldn't be here if it wasn't for me."

"Yes, you owe me now. Send some gold back to my family. The old woman with the quesadilla, she is my mother. Remember to write Penal Code 34 s1 (e), unauthorised entry and exit, so they will know what it is for."

"I will."

"Don't sob. You need a better back bone if you are going to have a greedy heart. See I told you; you are not doing this for greed, you are doing it to see if you husband lied to you on his death bed."

"Don't speak about him now. Not like this. At least you and I were honest about what we wanted. I am going to get that gold, make amends to people he wronged, to you and for Lucy. Then I will buy my freedom."

"Ah there it is, that look of elegant steel, like those gun slingers in the old movies. You will need that now. The Sheriff won't stop. You're a criminal like the rest of us in the law's eyes. You will need a strong heart and clear mind to buy your freedom from the Sheriffs."

He leant back on the sand and died.

She sobbed as the same hollowness she felt when Jack had died filled her. She had barely known this man, but he had been willing to risk his life to buy a chance at something better. She pulled some sand over Juan's body and took his sack. It was bright yellow leather with an embroidered Palma Verde tree on it. It was framed in an intricate border of red yarn. She saw he had a gun. She put it in her belt and took his food and water. She attached the pack to her own.

"Who made this Juan, your mother, a wife?" her eyes welled with tears with the sorrow of it all. She had lost everything and now she thought somehow that gold was going to fix it. Perhaps it would, after all that was what the world wanted now. That's how everyone paid for the privilege of being alive. Somehow the world put you in debt when you didn't even ask to be born in the first place. A quote came to her from a book she once read, a writer from a place called Cuba, "*No one should have to grovel for their life, like life was a favor.*" Reinaldo Arenas was his name. It was from many hundreds of years ago, but the data leaflet had slipped off a shelf in an archive bank, when she had to clean just to buy groceries. Those words remained with her, as the anger and bitterness of everything that had happened after Jack died. She had read his story and realised she needed to find freedom, or she would die.

The outline of the old speed rail car was black against the sands of the desert. It had come into

Anne's view as she had reached the top of a dune four days later.

She looked behind her. The seam of the horizon stitched to the sun by a cerise dusk was empty of her pursuer.

She focused her eyes at the half-buried rail car. It was unimaginable that there had been a railway leading to a city in this part of the world. It had become a radiation wasteland after a large satellite dish had crashed a few years after the great collapse.

She strode toward the carriage jutting vertically out of the dune. The entrance had been half torn open leaving a ragged slit a foot wide. She pulled on the edge of the door. It didn't budge. She took off her backpack. She gouged into the sand to loosen the door. Reefing the door again she managed to widen the gap. She flicked on her wrist tag light and peered in. The cloth of the seats had disintegrated leaving the platinum frames exposed. She saw the chest upside down at the bottom. She got her bearings and flicked off the light. She looked around for any movement.

She stumbled towards the treasure. Her foot hit something. She crouched down and felt the outline of the square box. She moved her fingers toward the front; the lock was still on it. Pulling out her knife she levered it into the lock and wrenched hard. It snapped easily weakened from the years of sand erosion.

"You know you will die here. The radiation will poison you." The Sheriff's voice spooked her. She turned frantically to see if he was here. But there was nothing. It was just her mind playing tricks.

She pried the lid open and flicked the light on. There it was. The treasure after all these decades; a dozen bars of gold.

Gold one of the last forms of free currency from the past millennia that still had value; rarer than any other mineral now; even this would have been melted down from reclaimed jewellery and coins of deceased estates.

She took the gold and stuffed it into Juan's pack. She felt her way to the entrance. She would need to wait until sunrise to begin her trek again.

Settling into the sand just inside the carriage she let her mind wander. It was finished. What would she do? The gold was hers and it was her ticket to a new life. Could she live without Lucy? She had for the last five years. The girl would be ok. Even Lucy had denied her parents when she enrolled at college. A prospector and a laundry woman for parents, didn't sit well with her college friends. She had sold their house to pay for Lucy's admission, she didn't owe the girl anything more. Those years had shown her what a person with money could do to survive and what a person without money needs to do. Both had left a bad taste in her mouth, but it would be wasted to just give gold back to a bank. It wasn't going to bring those people back her husband had killed. But she couldn't let it sit here and not at least try to break free of the chains that had destroyed her life. Besides there were people who now knew there was something worth looking for in the Arizona fall zone. No, the only one she felt an obligation to was Juan. He had helped her when no one else would and his price was reasonable so that it didn't break her back to pay it.

It was so silent. She had warmed to the impermeable darkness of the night desert. It meant that nothing could watch her, and she could forget about the rest of the world. Even the sound of her swallowing echoed into the night. The words of her last employer came to her as she had handed over her meagre wage "The problem with money, is once you get some you want it to be worth something, otherwise it's pointless and makes you realise how absurd life can be. Money isn't worth anything now, as you can't buy the things you really want." Anne remembered how much the woman had stashed in a safe. She had walked away thinking you obviously think it's still worth something. She fell into sleep with a thousand possibilities in her mind but only the emptiness of death and greed for the gold filled her heart. Was this what Jack felt every night he fell to sleep beside her she wondered. Did she and Lucy ever really mean anything to him? I guess he didn't have to tell her about the gold she dozed off consoling herself with this thought.

The dawn had barely broken when her eyes flew open. She had gotten used to sleeping with one eye open but not this time. She had gone into a badly needed deep sleep. She waited to see if she heard anything. Then slowly she peered through the crack in the door. She looked in the early morning light; nothing just dunes. She sat back and took another sip of water and ate some oat cake. She waited until it was fully light then went to the door again. She cocked her gun and poked her head up. Easing out her eyes darted from side to side. She looked at the sand for any footprints. She only saw her own.

She took out her phone and flicked the compass. North lead directly to the radiation hotspot. West was a thousand miles of desert and would kill her. East she would end up back at Bone Town.

South, the blackout zone started at Cuidad Obregad only one hundred miles away. It would be safe. She would send some money back to Juan's family when she reached there.

She hoisted the backpack and steadied herself against the weight of the gold. At least the desert was not hot, it was dry but not hot. The radiation layer that sat as a cloud over the region blocked the ultraviolet of the sun, so where a traveller may survive from the cooler temperatures it was the lack of moisture and radiation exposure that wrote their funeral dirge.

By midday she had walked ten miles only another ninety she thought. She sat to rest and ate some more oat cakes. At least with the

Juan's stash she would have enough food and water to just make it to the edge of the fall zone.

Another sunset threatened the sky, and the air suddenly grew colder. She checked her compass; she was on track.

She walked until the darkness returned and then she slept. Juan was talking to her in her dream then Lucy and then Jack on his death bed. She drank gold from a bottle and her heart filled with the liquid treasure and the lust for the freedom it would bring flowed like the sand dunes of the desert. Juan's voice floated in her mind 'Its unstoppable that lust sometimes. Its why the Sheriff follows. He knows the hearts of humans better than anyone.'

She woke suddenly on the dawn.

She began to walk again. It was another three days she calculated. A buzzard flew overhead. She looked up and followed it as it swept to her left. Her eyes caught the glimpse of the black hat as it bobbed for a split second above a distant dune. He was at least a day behind her. She looked behind her. Her footsteps were being erased by the small constant zephyr that tickled the sand grains.

It was two days later and in the shimmer of the sand haze she could see the outpost of the border. A sign showed it was ten kilometres to Hermosillo Town.

A shot rang past her suddenly. She fell to the ground and pulled out her gun. She aimed but the head disappeared behind a small rise. The weight of the gold lay on her back like the Sheriff. The head appeared she fired. Nothing happened. It just melted a strip of sand to glass. It wasn't a gun but a laser cutter. Juan must have brought it to cut up the gold.

She got up and began to run. It was now or never. The shots fired again but kept missing her. She wondered why his aim was so poor.

The fence marking the end of the fall zone was nearing. On the other side was the outpost marking the new territory of the Mexico Nation. Once beyond it she was outside his jurisdiction. She heard the galloping.

Run she thought. Juan's face rose before her. It spurred her on.

"Whatever you may judge mister I know this is only fair. I would make it right for me, Juan and those people who were killed. I am no thief or killer. I did what I had to do. You make nothing right in the world. You only make it more difficult to live."

She heard his voice again. The smooth self-assurance pierced the silent air.

"Ma'am I will shoot to kill on my next shot. Stop now. Your foolishness will cost you your life.'

The outpost was only another hundred paces away. She found the razor wire and slid under it. Her shirt caught on the hook of the post, it ripped the cloth and her skin. The Sheriff got off his horse and just stood there. His gun glinted like the badge on his chest. His face was once again hidden by shadow.

She flew through the wire, blood gushed as flesh caught on the barbs. She got out and bolted toward the bushes on the side of a road. She heard something coming. She dared to look over her shoulder. The Sherriff had turned and was going away from the fence. She saw a box truck coming along the road. She waved to it. The blink streak flashed signalling its intent to stop.

"Please I need a ride to the city centre." Anne wheezed. A man and a woman looked at her and the blood covering her hands and legs.

"Please" she pleaded "I can pay."

"In the back" spoke the man.

"Here for your cuts. The wire is lethal to many" the woman spoke as she handed Anne a towel.

"Thankyou" Anne almost cried. She scrambled onto the tray and hid beneath the sides. She couldn't see the Sheriff.

She dabbed at her cuts and tied the cloth around a deep gash in her calf. She took out the gun and one of the bullion bars. Using the laser, she cut the bar in half and then into sixteenths. She hadn't even thought of needing a tool like this. She put a piece in her pocket and stashed the rest in the pack.

The box car stopped suddenly. "Come we in the city" the man called to her. Anne got out.

"I need somewhere to stay before I leave so I can buy supplies. Is there an exchange?"

"Try Haspanas, it is a hostel. There is an exchange just over there." Anne gave him a piece of gold.

"Thankyou." He took it and whistled. He tipped his hat and got into the truck.

Anne picked her pack up and went toward the exchange. There was a line up outside.

"I am going to faint if I stay too long here. She tested her bottle, and it was empty. She saw a bubbler and went to it. Filling her bottle, she drank it empty and filled it again.

She waited on a bench, and saw the line dwindle. Getting up she joined in behind a woman and her two children.

"How much for a piece of gold?" asked Anne. The man behind the counter looked at her without expression. She placed a piece of the cut bullion in the drawer for him to inspect.

He picked it up and placed it inside a spectrometer to test its quality.

"Not bad, but I will have to report it. Its quality hasn't been seen around here for decades. Anything before fifty years has to be registered."

"Ok, but how much?"

"Two thousand."

"Ok"

"I'll need your name and details. And you will have to go to the Sheriff's office so your credentials can be checked. You know in case you stole this."

"Sheriff?"

"Yeah, and that could be a while. He would be in Bone Town for the festivals"

Anne's heart sank.

"What do you mean isn't this in the free zone?"

"Used to be, but the Sheriff purchased the land this side of Copper Canyon a few years back. We needed the money and juice from the network."

Anne's mind raced frantically.

"Ok if you give me twelve hundred can you overlook the paperwork. I am in a hurry and only passing through."

"The problem is how do I explain how I got hold of this piece?" The man looked at Anne and she knew he knew that she had met the Sheriff.

"Ok one thousand and I am sure you know ways to get paid in full without the Sheriff knowing about it."

"Ok." He took out a chip.

"Some coins as well" spoke Anne

She grabbed the chip and coins and left.

She went into a side street and sat down catching her breath.

"Ok calm down. Think. Get food, water, and map. I need to find where the free zone starts. It's the only way."

She walked again out into the main plaza. She saw a small shop still open. She went inside and grabbed some bottles of water and a few packets of energy bars. There was a woollen shawl with a hood. She took it as well. She saw a map key and grabbed one.

Three hundred rang up on the chip. Stepping outside again she chewed on a bar and swigged water. Looking at the map key she saw that heading southwest led to a blackened part of the map. It must be where the surveillance ends, she thought. The blackout cut through a place called Copper Canyon. The name sounded familiar. She flicked through her memories, and it came to her. She smiled. Anne tapped her finger on the map. That was the place to go she thought.

"Look, what's he doing here. Normally he is away at the festivals."

Anne heard two women speak as they left the shop.

She looked up and saw the Sheriff walking into a building across the other side of the plaza. Her heart stopped. She swigged the last of the water and put the hooded shawl on and covered her head. She began to walk along the road out of the town. It was at least three days to the Canyon. Once she passed the last house she began to run. Every pounding step on the road sent spikes of pain into her legs. The darkness came but she decided to keep going. In a blind panic she didn't notice the set of lights coming behind her until they were on top of her. She fell over thinking it was the Sheriff and rolled into the bushes.

The vehicle stopped.

"Hello, are you ok?" the voice was a woman.

Anne stayed still among the bushes.

"Hello is anyone there. Are you ok? Sorry I didn't see you until it was too late."

"Hello, sorry I am here."

Anne stood and saw the woman with her two children from the exchange.

"Are you ok? It is too dark here on the road at night."

"I realise that now but was anxious to keep going."

"I remember you from the exchange." The woman shone her phone light up at Anne.

"Yes, that is right. Which way are you going?"

"I am going to Chihuahua City."

"Can you drop me near Copper Canyon? I can pay you" asked Anne.

'Hop on. I am Maria and this is Rosa and Luca. I'll take you to San Juanita. It's only a few miles from the canyon."

"Thank you, Maria. I am Lucy." Anne saw the two children asleep in a side carriage.

They sped off. Anne clutched the handles on the back seat.

"Maria how far is it to the freezone?"

"Once you reach the canyon, just the other side is free or neutral. You need to reach Durango to be free of the Sheriff. He can't pass over the silent zone. It screws with their compasses."

"Ok what about bandits?"

"The Sheriff took care of them but once you are in the free zone then it will be different."

"When did it become part of the regulated territories?"

"Along time ago. I was only a girl. We ran out of signal and the crime escalated as people were being killed for their minerals. My mother said there were streets lined with barrels of dissolving bodies. The Sheriff came in with an offer we couldn't refuse."

Anne didn't answer her back. She remembered Bone Town and wondered if the people here knew what they were getting themselves into.

"Are there any border checks into Durango? I mean can people move freely into that part of country."

"Yes, but you need to be careful. There are no protections and not many rules. So, it is at your own risk. You will live or die by your own choices. It's the rules of the food chain. The apex predators dictate the laws."

"I understand" replied Anne.

She thought about what Maria said. She didn't say anything about how sometimes people learning to make their own choices is how things got better. To remain living under somebody else's rules can make things worse in the long run. It turned me into a murderer. No, you turned yourself into a murderer because you didn't want to live by somebody else's rules she thought. She shut her mind down. There was no good way, only the best way you can choose at the time when there are Sheriffs making the laws and the laws are unreasonable.

The dawn rose again. This time instead of grass plains there were rocky outcrops with brushwood trees. Hills were dotted with white square buildings made from old fashioned stone and mud rose in the distance.

"That is San Juanito" spoke Maria. She pulled over at a market stall.

"We can have some breakfast. I will rest for a little while and then leave for Chihuahua."

"OK I can buy some food if you like" Anne replied.

They ordered some burritos, coffee and bought some apples. Maria woke her children to eat.

"Over there, Mummy, there is a swing."

Anne looked across and saw a small park which had some tyres hanging from branches of a large fig tree.

The group strolled over. The kids quickly ate and drank and ran off to play.

"Where are you from Lucy?" Maria asked suddenly.

"North, San Fran."

"And you?"

"Chihuahua, a burb in the south."

"Are you on your own?"

"No. My wife lives there."

"How do you live?"

"This is my job. I courier parcels between three cities. My wife works away in the registry offices in Honduras which is why I bring the children. It will be hard in a year or two as Rosa will start late school and I won't be able to take them on my trips. Do you have a husband and children?"

"Used to not anymore. Just trying to start again. My name is Anne, Lucy is my daughter's name."

Maria nodded as she ate the burrito.

"Well Anne I am tired and would like to rest before I finish my trip. If you need medicine, there is a Pharmacia over there" Maria looked at the blood on Anne's pants.

"Thanks, I will. Which way do I go to get to the crossing over the canyon?"

"Take road sixteen south fork. You will a sign for the old San Rafael hotel."

Maria sat back against the tree and closed her eyes.

Anne took out five pieces of gold and placed them in her hand.

"I hope that helps for when Rosa needs to start school."

Maria looked at it surprised.

"Thanks, it will. Lucky we are here and not Durango. You would be killed for all your loot Anne. But here the Sheriff would know if any of his citizens had so much loot, they could spare that much for a stranger."

Maria looked at Anne, and Anne realized her mistake.

"Don't worry I won't tell anyone. But be careful who offers help and who you feel sorry for in Durango. Even the people you think you may have helped, puts them at risk becoming a target" Maria chided.

"People have died because of my ignorance Maria."

"No doubt they have. The northerners have a way of ignoring things when it suits them."

Anne stood up and collected her pack. Weariness washed over her but the fear of the Sheriff reaching her again made her keep going. She walked off and did not look at Maria again.

The sign San Rafael Hotel was rusted, and pock marked with laser holes. She took the road that followed the arrow. Cracks worked their way along it for miles, deep enough to fit a person. It wouldn't be enough to stop the Sheriff's horse.

She walked in half a daze she was so tired. She stumbled on a rock, fell over and reopened the wound on her leg. She stopped to tie the bandage again.

The silence was blissful as the trees swayed gently. She sat for a minute drinking water.

Suddenly the sound of hooves trotting broke the silence. They weren't close but she knew who they belonged to. Had Maria turned her in or did the Sheriff have some way of tracking her.

She got up and walked quickly. The derelict buildings of the hotel were obscured by overgrown trees. She walked into the foyer. She saw the sign and followed it. The trotting noise was closer.

She climbed through a window and half ran down the path toward the platform. She had remembered it from an old magazine. She thought how it would have been a great place for a holiday. A lot of fun. Now it was her only chance for escape.

The trotting had stopped.

A shot rang past her missing her again.

She ran toward the platform. The zipline sign was rusted like the jack attached to it. The line spanned across the canyon so far, she couldn't see the other side.

"You can't get me now. This is not your jurisdiction."

"Remember ma'am come this way again and there will be a warrant for your arrest."

"You need to learn justice sir, not just the law. You are no lawman you are like the man that half builds a house because to complete the whole thing means he needs to pay more tax if he finishes it. You have no sense of the social."

"Ma'am that gold was bought with blood, and it will bring only more blood on your hands. You should have let it lie. Sometimes the ends never justify the means."

"And what about that gold on your fingers. How was that paid for? What justice do you bring?"

She saw a smile rupture his face. "I am the bringer of law. Gold is the only thing equal in wealth to this knowledge. My citizens buy their lives with it. I buy mine with gold. It keeps my lithium batteries running now the satellites don't work. Besides Ma'am, you could've gone east or sent that money north like you said, but you ran south instead."

"You could have killed me back there? Why didn't you?"

"I hadn't warned you. Code 238 Penal Act 2190 three warnings maybe given in pursuit of a target. Then deadly force may be employed. In this jurisdiction four warning shots before a lethal one can be employed."

"Is it the gold the way you been tracking me?"

"Yes, it is ma'am. Now step away from the platform."

"The end may not justify the means Sheriff but for some there is no means and others are not allowed to choose their own end."

She took two pieces of gold out of her pocket and flung them at the Sheriff.

"That's one debt paid for. It is for the woman selling quesadillas and coffee. Penal code 34 section 1 (e) fine for unauthorized entry and exit."

She had one hand on the flying fox holster. She leapt up and pushed herself out over the platform. Below was a gorge five hundred feet deep. She sped away watching the figure beneath the black hat shrink. A fifth shot fired around her missing her again. The relief in her heart was as strong as the hope that the line did not break, and the Sheriff's aim did not improve.

Abundance

John Lee Hooker played on the radio in the bar. It was her favourite song. She hummed as the chorus began '*Well Mama killed a chicken, thought it was a duck, bundle up n go.*' It helped passed the time. The man on top of her was heavy and stunk. He stopped suddenly. The hand slapping her face made her ears ring drowning out the song's harmonica solo. He got off and left a few credit chips.

She staggered as she got up. Her face throbbed. She washed the blood and smell off her in the water bucket left at the door by the Saloon owner. In the background a song about peace and love started to play. It irritated her even more than the last client. Peace and love, yeah in another life. Nothing loving about Renaldo's gun pressed into her face demanding his money for the day's work.

She dressed and went out into the twilight glad to be out of there and away from the insipid whining coming from the radio. She saw a woman walking along the street.

"Where am I?"

"You are in Little Honduras."

"I need to find a doctor."

"You got to pay lady for that sort of information."

The woman didn't say anything. Treaszhur looked at her, the woman's skin was peeling, and she was stick thin.

The woman pulled a pack off her shoulder. Treaszhur saw something bright dazzle inside the bag as the woman opened it. Suddenly the woman produced a small pouch. She placed it in Treaszhur's hand.

They both looked at each other with equal pity and loathing. Treaszhur did not look away at the steel glare coming from the pale eyes of the woman. She knew she saw the red swollen cheek and lip. Treaszhur saw an emptiness behind the glare.

"Keep goin' that way. There is a guest house with a bar and should be a docta somewhere nearby."

Treaszhur walked on quickly hiding the pouch inside her bodice hoping that no-one had seen the woman give it to her.

Treaszhur reached her home, a humpy made from four sheets of aluminium. The code for the satellite it had fallen from had worn away leaving only the white façade of the cone shaped tail.

"Here ya go." She threw a small piece of bread to a stray dog that lived in a crate next door.

She went inside and wedged the door shut with a steel rod.

She sat on the bed. She opened the pouch and dropped the gold pieces into her palm. She pressed a piece between her fingers and then took a steel rod and struck it hard against the piece of gold. The rod bounced off and the piece pinged into the wall. Her heart thudded. If Renaldo found this, he would kill her trying to find out where she got it from. She lay back on the bed. She remembered the dazzle that came from inside the woman's backpack. She must have a bag full of it.

Renaldo would come after dark to collect his fee. She needed to be free. She had smelt her death nearing. At one time she was able to pass as an expensive call girl but now Renaldo only let her have the dregs. She wasn't educated to make use of her in any other way. It was time to leave. The lyrics *'Bundle up n' go'* played over and over in her head. *'Go on get get woman!'* chorused the throaty voice of John Lee Hooker.

She packed her bag and threw a shawl over her face. It was a three day walk to Honduras. The few dollars she made today would buy enough food until she could sell the gold.

Outside the darkness prowled around her but she was grateful for its protection from being seen. Reaching the freeway, she walked along the edge constantly checking behind her. She was making good time with no sign of anyone following, especially Renaldo.

The outskirts of Honduras City neared on the fourth day. Dusk descended quickly followed by nightfall. She turned and saw some headlights. She ran into the ditch beside the road. She peered up and sure enough the blue jacket of Renaldo reflected in the dim light. Why do you care so much dog? I am worth nothing to you she thought as the headlights of his bike kept sweeping over the ravine. He gave up after what seemed a lifetime to Treaszhur. She watched his bike disappear back in the direction it had come from.

The bustle of Honduras City was overwhelming. Treaszhur had only been here once as an escort for one of the Judges of the sector. That was when she was eighteen years old; almost thirty years ago. Her memories of the noise and lights emerged again as she entered the metropolis.

The sign to Sanctuary appeared on the main boulevard called the Road to Freedom. It sat beneath a cracked statue of Our Lady of Guatemala. This was where she needed to turn to reach her destination. Renaldo had often spoken of being able to buy and sell stuff in this part of the city. He would often say a prayer to lady liberty for good luck and fair game. She followed the boulevard until shacks lined the road.

The Judge told her of Sanctuary's history as a refugee camp formed after the great catastrophe. The people who lived here were descendants of northerners who had fled the storm of the satellites. His grandmother had been born in Sanctuary. He often boasted his family were some of the few to make it out of the constitution of poverty.

Dogs and kids littered the streets along with piles of electronic wires and microchip fragments. She went toward a queue of people in front of a shed made from steel beams and hessian cloth.

She slid in at the end of the line. She stared at nothing and spoke to no-one. Her face hidden like many of the others around her.

"Yes?"

"How much for this and need it in legit coinage."

She handed over a piece of gold.

The man eyed her suspiciously. In Haitian he called another man over.

They spoke for ten minutes with no indication that they were going to finish soon. A long line of people had built up behind her. If she didn't do something it would draw attention to herself.

"C'mon man, hurry it up. People are needin' to live 'til they die" she spoke urging the man to hurry up.

"Yeah, we can go to Ganga man, we're doin' you a fava" someone shouted behind her.

The man came back with a bag and some credit chips.

"Five hundred. If you want more you will need to go to Ganga, but he is more legit than us. Ya know what I mean. The judges will hear about it, ya know, only deals with the big fish ya know, he is a piranha to the shrimp."

"Yeah, I get it." She took the coins and chips.

Soaking in the bath she blanked her mind from the intrusions of Renaldo. She hadn't felt warm water over her body and the calming smells of lavender and rose in almost twenty years.

There was a knock on the door.

"Leave it in the room."

She heard the door close again. She got out of the bathtub. Her mouth and stomach grumbled at the smell of the eggs and pastries wafting into the room.

She pulled on a soft cotton gown and sat down to eat.

She cried as she ate. Stale bread and beans had been her food for decades. As the richness of the breakfast slid down her throat, she decided she would get healthy and then figure out what to do.

Treaszhur went shopping. She picked out a new dress, underwear, and shoes. Blue suited her complexion the best. She sat waiting for the assistant to finish packing her purchases. She flicked through a magazine. Her eyes scanned the perfect images. One caught her attention; a picture of a pristine beach and village set into a cliff. A meniscus of azure ocean surrounded the scene.

"Yes, isn't it gorgeous. Little bit o' Paradise it's called. Not often places there come up for sale. Like usually someone needs to die. If only I had that sort of money that's where I would be" spoke the shop assistant.

Treaszhur fingered the page staring at the blue ocean in the picture.

"Do you mind?" gesturing to take the magazine.

"Why of course ma'am. It's all yours."

Sitting on the chaise in her room she placed the code at the bottom of the picture under the scanner.

"Welcome to Little bit o' Paradise. How may I help you?"

"I'd like to view the places in your advertisement."

"Yes ma'am. When can we arrange a time?"

"I'm coming from Honduras City, so what is the best way to get there?"

"Well, you would need to travel to Itinerant City and catch ferry five from wharf two. It will bring you directly to Curacao Island. So how about we make an appointment in three days, so you have a day to rest and look at things for yourself before we meet."

Treaszhur swallowed hardly able to contain herself.

"Yes, that would be good."

"You have our location?"

"No can you tell me?"

Treaszhur hung up and began packing. She managed to catch the six o'clock train out of Honduras. She kept repeating ferry number five, wharf number two to herself. It would save her having to ask someone which boat to get.

The boat nudged the jetty. The air was like nothing she had ever smelt. Not even the perfumes and soaps she had been bathing in for the last few weeks matched the dance of the ocean breeze that played across her flesh.

She walked along the boardwalk and saw the white lacuna of sand in the distance. The waves were gentle in their kneading. Little white cottages dotted the shoreline and cliff side. She smiled broadly and deeply. Her home could be here. For some strange reason, the little dog at her humpy came to mind. Tears welled slightly. She should have taken it with her.

She went to a small cottage where a sign with a picture of a bed and meal hung outside. She went in. The bedroom for rent was a small attic converted with enough space for a double bed, chair, and tallboy chest of drawers. She placed her bag on the chair and looked out the circular window toward the beach and ocean.

Strolling along the beach the salty smoothness of the waves sliding over her feet was like the eggs she ate every morning. Suddenly a great fatigue moved in on her like tropical storm clouds nearing the coast. Her shoulders sagged and she had to sit down. She breathed in and out and felt every particle of air abrade her throat and lungs. She was alive and free. Everyone she had ever known was dead or dying of the life they had been forced into. Life now was as dilapidated as the space junk that formed the architecture of the humpies she had lived. A home made from crumbs of memories and dreams that spilled over drowning the hearts and imaginations of those born later into cradles of dead metal and a destroyed earth. Except here, here Treaszhur saw the promises that history tried to make come true and the possibility of dreams being real.

"Now ma'am in what manner will you pay for your deposit?"

"Oh, I will pay for the whole thing with coinage."

The young woman smiled at the commission she would make.

"Now I just need papers verifying your identity ma'am."

Treaszhur didn't say anything. Her heart felt like it would burst with disappointment.

"If I said to you that I have no way of verifyin' who I am as I lost it all in a fire many years ago… is there another way. I mean I am willin' to pay."

The girl smiled at her.

"Well ma'am, you see the difference is that in the north some way of negotiation could be entertained but here they are strict. The people here know they have the best bit of the entire world and want to keep it that way."

"I understand." Treaszhur did understand. It was the detritus of the world like herself that was clogging everything including the ocean. She knew it was not her fault, but it was just simply that's what life had become.

"Is there another way you accept payment besides bein' verified? I mean the smell of the ocean, I've never…"

"We can accept papers from a sheriff or judge who has known you for at least five years. We need to be strict ma'am you understand. The papers need to be legit as forgery incurs a large fine. The papers need to contain the exact codes and statutes indicating that you have been associated with either a sheriff or judge for five years. If you were verified, then you would still need sign off from a sheriff or judge, but it can be done in the courthouse offices. But because you aren't then it's different. You understand."

The girl looked at Treaszhur sensing the dilemma and disappointment that lingered. She saw the scarred knuckles from the punishments over the years. She knew what lay within this woman's grasp and the desperation of seeing salvation just within reach.

"Once payment is made how long until final payment is required with the paperwork?" asked Treaszhur.

"Well, there is no time limit. The only thing that will change is if someone comes along with full payment and papers, they will take ownership. Of course, your money is refunded."

"Ok here is the payment in full. I will be back."

The girl wrote out the receipt and stamped it.

As Treaszhur made her way back to the hotel she saw a crowd gathering in the street. There was someone screaming. She stopped and peered through the spectators.

"Put your weapon down sir. Let the woman go or I will shoot."

"Why do you care so much about a whorin witch like this one?"

"Sir you are placin' yersself in a precarious position. Put the weapon down or I will shoot."

Suddenly a loud bang echoed so strongly that Treaszhur felt a blow to her chest. The taser gun had gone off and the man dropped to the ground. The girl ran to the Sheriff, and he grabbed her as she collapsed.

"Now, now, it's over. Just you stay there. Deputy, go ask the women from the Lost and Desperate shelter to take this girl, give her a meal, and bed for the night. She mustn't be any more than fourteen years old."

Treaszhur looked at the lawman's hand stroking the sobbing girl's soft brown hair. It reminded her of the little dog she used to pet, its desperate eyes pleading for any bit of affection and kindness.

"He's dead Sheriff" spoke one of the other Deputies.

"Too bad, don't believe in killing but he wouldn't listen."

"He's a good'un compared to the last one. Particularly if the pimps been beating on us. Wonder how long this one will last? The Judges get nervous if the Sheriffs are bein' too friendly."

"Yeah, he just started here, which means if he doesn't get killed, we have ten years of a little slice of heaven ladies."

"Yeah, he's runnin' the jailhouse like a guesthouse even if you're on death row. Almost worth turnin' yersself in."

"And give up hustlin' for a livin,' young man you need your head read."

The group broke into hysterical cackling as they walked away from the scene. Treaszhur walked behind them. She knew the depth of relief that came when there was just the slightest chance of someone caring; even a little. She wondered about the Sheriff. She had only ever met Judges, never Sheriffs. They didn't care about people like Treaszhur.

Treaszhur drummed her fingers on the windowsill staring at the street full of people. Everyone looked poor to hide the fact that anyone who had money could avoid being robbed. She remembered the smell of the ocean. She decided to go for a day trip back to the bay and look at the ocean. Getting off the tram she brought a coffee and a gelatin donut. She strolled along the sea wall. Even though it was overcast the turquoise water was dazzling and begged her to go for a swim. She sat on a bench. A person came and sat down on the other end of the bench. They were well dressed to be strolling along the beach she thought.

"It's the best place to sit and think, isn't it?" they spoke suddenly.

"Yes, it is" she responded.

"I haven't seen you here before."

Treaszhur tensed slightly at the question.

"No, I have arrived recently. Took up some house cleaner work."

They nodded. "You smell nice for a house cleaner" they spoke grinning.

She saw the eyes and knew what they wanted. She looked at the cuffs with the brown and purple stripes on them. They pulled them down quickly to hide them.

"I like my perfumes. The ladies I clean for sometimes let me keep their leftovers" she replied.

"Perhaps we could spoil each other."

She looked at the Judge. Would they want to help her? She remembered the Sheriff he did something for nothing. The Judges understood a transaction, but their prices were steep, even lethal sometimes. Their ideas of freedom and justice were arbitrary in Treaszhur's experience. She had no gripe with them, but she was low down on the food chain, she was no threat to Judges. The Sheriffs were though, that's why the Judges kept a leash on them like everyone else. You never knew what a Judge's name was and you rarely saw the same one twice.

She looked back across the ocean. The vastness and freedom it offered without even needing to be part of it was still amazing to her. Until now she had only ever thought about getting enough to eat and pay Renaldo. Make it work. Make it work this time Treaszhur thought.

"Your Honour," she paused letting it sink in she knew exactly who they were, "I think you might be mistaken but unless you need cleaning services then I am not sure how else I can help you."

The Judge coughed realizing their mistake. They stood and walked away from her. She watched their back and saw that their head remained straight, not even turning once to look at the ocean.

Treaszhur felt the anger swell inside her followed by that sense of hollowness. When you were part of the unverified, you were never heard, never seen unless you had some use for the legit folk, even then they would discard you when they were finished. Even the law didn't want to know you, the unverified were accused of getting away with a lot, not because they had freedom, but because they weren't even recognized as human enough to do anything considered a crime. They were relegated to the dogs and cats of the slums and eradicated in the just the same way when their numbers swelled too much. Treaszhur took deep breaths to calm down. The image of her friend Karin lying dead in the gutter one morning after a purge had haunted Treaszhur for the last twenty years. Karin had been an older woman who had looked after her when she was new to the business. Treaszhur had known in that instant, where her future lay. That was why the Judges used them, they knew using the unverified left no crumbs to lead back to their law breaking.

"Make it work this time" she spoke to the ocean.

Treaszhur got up and walked back to find the tram. She noticed a bar. It had the same symbol as the one in Little Honduras where she had told that woman to go for help. She decided to get a drink before going back.

"I'll have a Pimm's and Tequila chaser."

"That's five hundred" spoke the bartender.

"Sheesh its steep here honey." Treaszhur realized she didn't have enough coins to pay. She fingered the small pouch. She took out a chip which had been melted down from one of the gold lumps.

"Will this do?"

"Yishoti, can you look at this?" called the bartender.

A man came out and took the piece of gold. He looked at Treaszhur. He went into a room.

"Yeah, its fine. Open a tab if the lady wants."

Treaszhur went out to the terrace and watched the ocean again. The man came out smoking a cigar.

"Hello, do you know where I can find a courthouse?"

"No ma'am."

"Do you have a data-hub to look up where they might be?"

"There was another collapse of satellites over Colombia. It will be three days until there are any services" he replied.

"Ok. How do I get to the main plaza for the whole city from here?"

"Take the tram to Iguana Fall stop eight on red line. Walk directly north along Main Street and you will see it on top of the hill."

Treaszhur looked at him wondering if he was going to ask where she got the gold from, but he kept looking at the ocean as he smoked his cigar.

It got the better of her and she blurted out "Well ain't you gonna ask?"

The man looked at her "About what?"

"That bit of gold."

"If I asked every patron about how they managed to pay for their liquor I'd go out of business so fast it wouldn't be funny."

"Does that Judge come here often?"

"I haven't seen any Judges in here. They tend to keep to themselves."

"Do you have a place in Little Honduras?"

"I do." Treaszhur didn't say anything else in case it somehow got back to Renaldo where she was.

"I don't drink much, been more hungry than thirsty in my time. If you know what I mean?"

"That's fine, we serve food as well. Like I said you have credit here, anytime you want to drop by. It's always nice to watch the ocean." The man went inside again.

Treaszhur finished her drink and made her way back to the tram. She looked behind her to see if anyone was following but there was no one there.

When the tram came it was full and a long line was waiting for the next one. Treaszhur decided to walk. It was warm and the air fresher than usual. The road gently sloped up away from the beach. After five miles she walked past the statue of Our Lady of Guatemala and saw the road to Sanctuary again. Peering down the road, there was the usual queue at the Haitians exchange shed. She picked her pace up as she strode past the turn off to Sanctuary. Her suit while plain spoke of money compared to the people there. Soon she saw a spire in the distance. It was the cathedral on the hill. Its silhouette stood out like a beacon, empty now and only signalling as a tourist attraction. She remembered a Judge telling her when some agreement had been made a long time ago, the churches were deemed foreign to the lands here and told to close. The buildings were kept but adherents to them were told to find their own way. The Judge said they knew the human heart better than anyone and said any path to truth had to come from an open mind and self-reflection. The Sheriffs closed the churches after that. Still there were pop up faith groups here and there but they didn't last because they couldn't accumulate any money as the Sheriffs always knew where the money was and would break them up. Treaszhur remembered a few of them used to help the people like her but usually the help came with a price. You had to believe in gods and spirits. To Treaszhur it felt like another set of laws like the ones that ignored people like her. Still there were ones who were very kind and left food and clothes from time to time. She remembered any that tried to help anyone leave, seemed to disappear, and never returned. It was like they were being watched as well.

Puffing she sat down on a bench. She saw a person with a yellow pack. It caught her eye. The person turned around and she saw it was the same woman who had given her the gold. Treaszhur placed a scarf over her face to stop her recognizing her. She watched the woman walking half dazed as she stopped people to speak to them and then give them one of her pouches.

"You gonna get yourself killed lady" Treaszhur spoke.

The woman walked off down the road toward the western edge of the city. Treaszhur lost sight of her.

Treaszhur continued into the plaza and saw the courthouse. There were guards either side of it and people being checked as they went inside. She strode inside. A glass petition sectioned off the town clerks.

"I'd like to know find out how I can ask a Judge or Sheriff to assist with providing verification?"

The clerk looked at her blankly.

"You will need to be identified first to be verified. Name and gestation completion date?"

"Maya Tresor, 29 February 2474."

The screen flickered as the clerk swiped over the surface entering the details. She scrolled a few pages.

"No there is no record here under that name or gestation date. It's probably because you were born on 29 February. It was a glitch in the program. It didn't register any bioforms during the initial upgrade phases on your arrival date occurring in a leap year."

"What do you mean? There must be some record of me, I am here."

"Are you sure those are your details?" the clerk asked genuinely wanting to help.

"They are the only things I have always known. My name, the day I arrived and that I am alive."

"I checked again there is no one on our records of that name or date."

"Is there some way of getting verified without being identified?"

"No but I will check with my supervisor."

The clerk walked over to a person sitting at a desk. The other person nodded. Treaszhur noticed the datahubs were working here. The man at the bar had said it would take three days for the connection to restored.

"If you don't have any identification than you aren't verified and can't obtain verification even from a sheriff or judge" spoke the clerk.

"I was told I could get some verification for a purchase?"

"I don't know who told you that, but you might want to ask for your money back. Places like Sanctuary might be able to help you."

"Well, there must be some ways of getting identified?"

"Look if you do some research, the library has archives, you could see if there is some old statute or something which might help you. We only have current rules so I can't look it up for you. You need to do it yourself. If you find something, then you need to fill in one of these forms with submissions to obtain a court date. But otherwise, I can't help you."

"But I can't read or write. You must be verified to get educated."

The woman looked at her blankly. Treaszhur wasn't sure if it was to be sarcastic, like why don't you understand anything, or it was incomprehensible to her what Treaszhur had just said.

"You can take box tram thirty-one, get off at stop twenty. You will see the library. Next."

The clerk cut Treaszhur off not that she had anything else to say.

She went across to the tram tracks and waited near the speaker to hear tram thirty-one being announced. It took an hour for a tram to come. She watched the streets pass by and saw people wandering around aimless in their purpose and directions. Mostly they were alien to her the people here. They didn't see people like Treaszhur, the law didn't recognize them so neither did they. Even the faith folk picked and chose who they saw. And why did the Courthouse datahubs work and not the bar? She felt the purse hidden under her bodice. The gold was probably stolen. And it would incur questions as to how a non-verified suddenly got enough money to get verified. It might be a freezone in name, but there were just as many rules to follow regardless of whether there were any sheriffs around. She would be sent straight back to Little Honduras, and Renaldo, not even the protection of a prison awaited her. She thought of the Sheriff in the street that day. He looked too honest to accept a bribe. He wouldn't help her, because he would stick to the law, and the law said, the unverified didn't exist, and so he couldn't even put her in prison without some identification.

"Make it work Treaszhur" she whispered.

"Stop 20" announced the tin mechanical voice.

Treaszhur got off and immediately ahead of her was a stone building. It had no signs only metal doors and long slit windows.

Inside was dark and cool. A faint musty odour permeated the air. It made Treaszhur nervous. She had been locked in rooms like this with perverts before. She wanted to run.

The woman at the library counter looked at her surprised. Normally no-one came to the library directly anymore. Mostly it was just a storage facility for records.

"Ma'am do you know of some way I can be educated on how to be verified?"

The woman looked intensely at her. Treaszhur couldn't figure out if it was surprise or suspicion.

"I can pay."

"That isn't something we get asked very often these days. You must be from out of town?"

"Yes I am."

"Well you will need to look in the Legal Statutes section. It's in floor three, row A to H."

Treaszhur hesitated. The old woman looked at her.

"Is something wrong?" the woman asked.

"Well to be honest, I can't read or write, and I need to learn to do that as well."

"Well you will be busy, won't you?" the old woman smiled.

"Do you know of somewhere I could learn?" Treaszhur asked.

"I have done some tutoring in my time and could help you out."

"Ok how much and how long do ya reckon?"

"I will do some tests, and let you know. I will need time to prepare a schedule. We have had a large shipment of archiving to do. Would you like some work to help you pay?" she asked. Her eyes were unreadable, a pale brown. Her black, grey hair was dull like her skin.

"I can't read or write lady. What good am I?"

"Just organizing to begin with but when it's time to label well we can use that to help with your learning."

"Ok so when can we start?"

"I finish each day at three pm. On Monday, Wednesday, and Fridays we can meet at the café around the back of the building. On the other days you can help me sort these boxes. Come back tomorrow at nine."

Treaszhur handed some coins over to the woman.

The librarian smiled. "You know I don't get paid to look after the archives. I do it simply because I love it. Also the Sheriffs would come nosing around if they found there was money being exchanged."

Treaszhur laughed "Babe, I worked all my life getting paid to give pleasure to strangers. I hated every second of it."

The house cleaner that came to clean Treaszhur's room saw paper notes covered in repeated letters and words stuck on every wall and table. She would see the woman who rented the room sitting in the tub talking aloud to herself. One day she heard '*Section 157 law code 1157 of the Sector Honduras: Any breaches of this incurs a ten-year penalty of incarceration and fines of up ten thousand coinage bits.*

Evidence served as part of a criminal charge is returnable as proceeds in the event that no claim of ownership is made in the time of incarceration'.

On another day there was a long piece of writing copied from an open tablet "*terminology related to the definitions of the Human Bioforms, Division 2 Part 2.3 subclause 1 (a)*"

"Well Maya, that is all I can teach you now. It has been a pleasure and with the year's tuition I am planning a holiday."

"Oh where?"

"I am going to travel to the southern tip of Ushuaia. I want to watch the icebergs float by and see the penguins and walruses that live there. Maybe meet a nice Chilean."

Treaszhur smiled. "Do you think money buys happiness?" she asked.

"Money buys choice, so if another option is happier for someone then yes it will."

"Yeah, I figured money is only half the story with happiness. I met a woman who gave me some coins virtually for free. I see her from time to time around the city. She was lost the first time I met her and still seems lost. Like she doesn't know what to do."

"Have you thought of speaking with her. She did help you."

"Hmm. I don't know. I just took it as a gift. I don't want to ruin the luck it has given me."

They stood up and Treaszhur was surprised that the old woman kissed her on the cheek. She placed a present wrapped in silicon paper in her hand. By its shape Treaszhur guessed it was a book.

"I noticed you borrowed this one the most. Good luck dear. I hope you get whatever it is you want."

Treaszhur sat in her room and pulled out the form from the courthouse. She neatly filled it in and signed it. Putting her coat on she went outside. The line in the courthouse was short today. She reached the counter within half an hour. She handed the form over. The clerk was a different one to the one she had spoken to before.

The clerk took it and checked all the details. Then he turned to the screen and scrolled through several pages.

"Ok the form is in order. I have booked your court hearing for three weeks' time. It will be Judge 28. You will need to prepare a written statement signed and dated and witnessed by someone you know. Hold your right wrist out."

He tattooed a small barcode on the underside of her wrist.

"Hello again, dinner?"

"Thanks, Yishoti. I'll have some frittata and a glass of Pimms."

"See you doing some more writing today?" Yishoti asked.

"Yes, and I have a favour to ask. I can pay."

"Yeah, sure shoot."

"Once I finish, I'll let you know. How is my tab going?"

"Well, your credit was used last month. It was twelve months altogether."

"Ok, here ya go, and it might cover the favour as well." Treaszhur handed over a small cube of gold. Yishoti placed it in his waist pocket and went into the kitchen.

Treaszhur put her note pad on the table and began to type:

"I Maya Tresor of gestation completion date 29 February 2474, seek dispensation to be identified.

I am seeking this dispensation so I may live as a free verified citizen in the state of Durango in the Equatorial Territories.

I have lived a life of hard work, endurance, tenacity and acted upon my circumstances when an opportunity arose. I have learnt to read and write this statement freely, and now wish to live freely within the laws and statutes of Durango State, signee to the Peace Act 2320 – Agreement to moving forward between the Human Bioforms and Cybernauts.

I seek leniency on this matter, as the situations and circumstances which led to my not being identified was out of my control due to a technical error in the programs which recorded my arrival into the world.

I believe I should not be impugned for the rest of my natural born life as a non-person because of this technical deficiency which denied recognition for this human bioform known as Maya Tresor.

By this action to seek validation and recognition of my person I bring the freshness of the novel and the new. A precedent to allow the unverified and non-identified to participate.

The potentialities which may arise from this action align with the Peace Act of 2320 whereby it was defined to be a human bioform was to act upon and within the world with a view of its future, an understanding of its past and the lessons learnt from it and provide promises to those who may come afterwards.

Freedom requires acknowledgement of the commune and society but also the darkest, loneliest, and most noble elements of every human heart and mind. This capacity for individuation and the social were defining elements of the human bioform. It is this which was not compatible with the formation of the Cybernauts and their capacity for integration.

The Cybernauts who through constant uploading of information developed the ability to know what was going to happen before it happened and wrote the laws to manage the future. But while these laws have some wisdom in them, they do not express the true essence and principles by which the treatise was enacted i.e. to acknowledge the concept of the "human condition" within the world which made it. This condition formed the pathway to a special mention afforded to the human bioform due to its longstanding history of surviving the inexhaustible efforts of nature to wear down the durability of all things constructed within the system called life.

By allowing a human bioform to continue in the shadows of existence and deny the historical narrative of any human to engage with the world fully, purely because of an arbitrary programming error formulated by regulations derived from the definitions of the first laws at the time of scribing the treaty, undermines the very principles it was attempting to enshrine as an authoritative framework for co-existence between the human bioform and the machine.

That is, the human bioform was made and exists within the engines of the natural and its purpose is to overcome the world and themselves. Its history and advancements bear witness to the seduction and solace of living a life free from the labour required to live. This concept brings both meaning and consciousness to the human bioform.

My life since birth was to engage in this very fundamental principle expressed above. That is to labour within the necessities of life driven by the coercion of nature to survive. I am the very definition of what it is to be the human bioform. This fact then ensures entitlement to the noble idea to seek freedom from the tyranny the system of life imposes on me until death takes me.

I have lived the very essence of a human bioform even with the superimposition of the data label nonperson, of no identification and no verification. This contradiction in terms undermines the very foundations on which the treaty was formulated and all that has been striven since its implementation.

In being denied this request for identification a grave breech of the precepts listed in Part 1 Act

2320 will be enacted. Thereby undermining the foundations by which the world agrees to live by, both human and machine.

In denying this request it condemns both human and machine to live under the tyranny of intransigent rules and regulations and prevents the rectification of errors and opportunity to bring new datum into the system called life. Additionally it denies opportunities and potentialities which are defined as forming the framework of the bioform called the human person as per section 6.4 subclause 2 (e) i.

To conclude, I, Maya Tresor, being a human bioform alive and present in the here and now, have a heart, lonely and happy at the same time but bursting with desire to be free of its condemnation at its birth by a mere technical blip.

Being identified means I can live this noble idea of freedom and participate to the fullest meaning of the human condition, first laid down by nature and again by the laws and governances of the Durango State signee of the Peace Act of 2320."

She put the tablet down. She finished her drink. She walked over to the office near the bar and knocked on the door. Yishoti answered it.

"Here to call in a favour."

"Come in."

She handed Yishoti the tablet.

"I need a witness for this submission to court. It needs to be someone I have known for twelve months. My hearing is next week."

Yishoti read it. He held the stylus in his hand poised ready to sign it. Treaszhur looked around the office. A large digital map showing freezones and blacked out areas spanned across one wall. On them sat small pulsing red dots indicating some sort of location. She noticed a detailed one of the city, and lots of dots clustered in various spots, especially the plaza. They were unlabelled. Treaszhur wondered what the nature of Yishoti's real business was.

"Impressive, just one question."

Treaszhur tensed thinking he would not sign it.

"The gold, it is a very rare purity for these days. Can I ask where you got it from?" Treaszhur's heart thudded wondering whether to be honest or not. It was a transaction like any other transaction. If she told, would he kill that woman who gave it to her. Would he come after her now that he had done something for her. She watched him sign the tablet before she answered. In that instant she thought Treaszhur you either learn to start trusting a future exists for you or go back to Renaldo now.

"I didn't know the woman's name. She was lost and gave me some for helping her. I only saw her once more and never again."

Yishoti handed the tablet back to Treaszhur.

"There you go Maya. As I said you have credit here whenever you want to drop in. Good luck."

Treaszhur took the tablet and left. Looking back, she checked to see if anyone was following her.

Judge twenty-eight looked across at Maya Tresor. The face was blank, and it was hard to discern if it was male or female, not that it mattered as Judges had no identities. It was to remove any sense of bias.

"Your identity is granted Maya Tresor. The technical error you have rightly pointed out for not allocating a bioform imprint, has since been rectified and no longer acts as a reason to deny identification. On this basis you have met the requirements for identification. Your record will reflect this decision as of this day 28 November 2523. Please go to the imprint office for the procedural requirements to have your record updated."

"You sure are pretty ma'am."

"Thank you. I am looking for the Sheriff's office."

"Just over there. And ma'am when you're finished, I am just here."

She nodded her head at the man. He was well dressed and very courteous.

She entered the Sheriff's office. One of the deputies looked up at her as she walked toward the counter.

He eyed her "Ma'am how can I help you?"

"I have a bag of gold I need to hand in. I was dealin' in some small amount. Nothin' much just so I can get well, cleaned up and hire an attorney."

"I see ma'am."

The deputy picked up the bag and looked inside. He lifted his eyebrows and whistled.

"Sheriff" he called.

The same tall thin man she saw over a year ago in the street looked at her and tipped his hat.

"What is it deputy?"

The deputy handed the bag of gold to him. He looked inside and then at Treaszhur.

"Is this yours' ma'am?"

"It is sir."

"Is it all you have ma'am?"

"Now it is. I sold a third in Sanctuary to get myself well and buy a little luxury before I die."

"I see. Where did you get it from?"

"A traveller. She paid me for some help I gave her in Little Honduras."

"Is that where you are from?"

"I am. I was a sex worker there."

"Now you understand that I will have to arrest you not only for possession of this but also for dealing in it."

"I know."

He eyed her suspiciously.

"Sir I intend to start a new life. I will pay my dues for this and then I know I can rest easy."

She put her bag down waiting to be taken into a cell.

"Hold your hand out." The Sheriff scanned her wrist. "Deputy start the paperwork." He took the bag away.

Treaszhur stood before the Judge.

"Five years ma'am. If the gold is unclaimed, it will be reimbursed to the defendant on discharge if there is a good behaviour recommendation." The gavel fell.

Treaszhur turned to her attorney.

"Thank you. I expect everything is order."

"Yes, it is."

The Sheriff placed the cuffs on her again and escorted her to the back of the courthouse where she would spend the next five years of her life. He hesitated as he closed the cell door.

"Ma'am I still shake my head at what you did. No one would have known about that gold further south than here. You could have been a very wealthy woman. Is there some reason you turned yourself in and don't tell me it's to make an honest woman of yourself?"

Treaszhur sat on the bed. Amongst the few comforts she was allowed to bring with her she saw the book the librarian had given her called Statutory Requirements for Retrospective Verification of the Human Bioform Part III – Proofs for verification. Just sticking out was the corner of the advert for a Little Bit o' Paradise.

"Well Sheriff maybe over the next five years we can get to know one another, and all your questions will be answered."

Ir Con la Botella

Corinne breathed in the warm air as she climbed out of the ocean and onto the shores of Cuba. The salty water ran off her skin down into the craggy rocks. She had jumped off the junk ship about twelve miles out to swim the rest of the way. She held her hand up against the horizon. There was three fingers width between the sun and blue line of the ocean. She estimated it was about an hour after dawn. Throwing her ruck sack over the stone wall she stood on the Malecon and looked left and right. There was no traffic. She remembered the address she had been given; cnr Concordia and San Rafael. She began to walk. The hot breeze quickly dried her clothes and her hair. Her mouth was parched from the salt water. She tested her water pouch, but it was empty.

Compared to the ocean littered with the dregs of the last satellite storm, the Malecon was like walking on silk. The buildings at the edge of the city rose above her but did not dominate the skies like they did in the north. Some of the old Spanish facades had been recently scrubbed back showing the white stone and old grandeur from centuries before. A bronze face looked at her as she entered the maze of terraced housing. It was a sculpture from long ago. She had seen this statue in its original glory. The trails of sculpted bronze elegantly disappearing into streamers had been worn down, but the details of the large face crowned with petals remained. Music played gently; it was Shostakovich whispering on the breeze. To hear its tones and lilting softness against the heat of the day was startling in its contrast. She decided to follow the sound as if it was water calling her to drink. The source of the music drew closer. Behind iron barred windows she saw a group of children in a ballet class. They were oblivious to her as they focused on their immature movements with perfect grace.

A taxi glided past; bright yellow and white, longer than a wave breaking on the sandy shore. She flicked through her memory banks, a 1960 Buick.

"Ride" called the driver.

She could ask for some bytes when she got to the house to pay him. Nodding she hopped in the back. He smiled at her with a mouth full of perfectly sculpted gold teeth.

She saw the miniscule chip in the incisor and power pack attached to the dash of the car. Clever she thought.

"I wondered how you were fuelling the car?"

"One smile can go a mile. Where to missy?" he asked.

The car moved forward along the street.

"Corner of Concordia and San Rafael."

He nodded. She scanned the rows of terrace houses looking for a green door.

"There" she pointed. The door was framed with two old men smoking. They tipped their hats to her as she got out.

"Wait here." She knocked on the door.

No one answered. The taxi driver waited patiently. He was lighting up a cigar.

It opened. A girl stood looking at her. She showed the card with the signature on it.

"I need two bytes for the taxi."

The girl darted into the darkness of the hallway.

"Rosa tell her to come in" called a woman's voice.

Corinne saw the silhouette of the girl's hand motioning for her to come in.

"Have you eaten?" asked a woman standing inside a kitchen at the rear of the house.

"No. I need to pay the taxi."

"Rosa has taken care of it. Take a seat."

Corinne threw her satchel down and pushed it between her feet as she sat at the table.

She saw a man sitting at the rear in the courtyard. He was reading. He looked up at her and nodded. She hadn't seen anyone from the western edges of the Pacific Ocean in decades.

"Who are you?" Corinne asked turning back to the woman.

"I am Maria."

Maria put a plate down in front of Corinne. She sucked down a glass of water and immediately poured another glass. Then began to scoff down the rice, beans, and chicken. Maria watched her.

Corinne realised she would need to be careful; the food was always rationed even in the approved tourist homes. She slowed her eating and stopped gulping the water.

Maria put a glass of lemonade on the table. Corrinne sipped on it; the acidity of the lemon felt like razor blades on her throat.

"Thankyou" she croaked.

"So, you got the stuff?"

"Maybe." Corinne eyed Maria closely through filaments of cigarette smoke. She didn't know this woman and she could be fishing. Spies everywhere.

"Don't worry. The reason I ask is that you need to keep it close. The Sheriff is looking for it. Came all the way from the fall zone in the north."

Corinne shivered slightly. She had heard of the Sheriff but never had any run-ins with him. He was a second-generation automaton following the singularity. They became the bridge between the first-generation Cybernauts and the human, until the third-generation hybrids were formulated. When flexible thinking was combined with biology and the capacity of quantum computing. Beings like Corinne; designed to rebalance the equation between the human and the machine. The only side effect was long lived cell memory prolonging life expectancy and slower aging. With it came amnesia though. To live so long and see the repetition of existence lead to depression but the quantum waves negated this effect embedding new mitochondrial reproductions instead of using old matter. The universe was saved again from complete exhaustion and monotony.

"Where is the safe house?" asked Corinne rousing from her memories.

"This is it. Didn't they explain anything to you before you left."

"Yeah, but it seems a bit obvious."

"Why?"

"I don't know. It just seems exposed."

"Can't see the forest for the trees, isn't that the old saying."

Corinne looked at some photos on the wall. They were of Maria and another woman with two children in front of a box motorbike. There were post-cards of Chihuahua City pinned randomly around the photo.

"When you are finished there is a room upstairs and some water to bathe. You're as crusty as the Malecon sea wall." Maria chuckled as she picked up a bag. "I'm going to the store."

"Who is the visitor?" Corrinne nodded toward the man sitting in the courtyard.

"That's Yishoti. You might find him interesting."

Corinne smiled looking at Yishoti as she munched on a drumstick.

"Rosa tell Luca to take his medicine when he gets home. I have left everything out for him. And both of you do your homework before dinner" called Maria as she strode toward the front door.

Corinne could hear Rosa playing a violin in the front room. The imperfect notes echoing around her mind and the house. She drank some more lemonade. Picking her pack up she went to her room. It was simple with a double bed and bathroom off the side. She stripped off and placed her clothes in the tub floor to wash them as she bathed. She saw a shirt and jeans hanging in the closet with a shawl made with red, blue, white, green, and yellow patches crocheted together.

On the tiled wall beneath the shower head was a cacophony of power packs and wires leading out into the bathroom and bedroom. It was an accident waiting to happen. She saw the eye of the satellite connection blinking yellow. Power hadn't been restored yet. She went to her pack and took out a small key-drive. She undid the wiring and reorganized the power packs so that they were flush against the wall and the exposed leads were safe away from the water. She then took a piece of string she had in her tool pack and neatly tied the power cables together and guided them over some nails sticking out. Satisfied it was neat and safe she put her tools back.

Stepping underneath the spray of water she washed the salt of the ocean away. A flash of the boat going down in water, aflame. It was the prison boat from Honduras taking her to Devil's Island. She had survived because she wasn't shackled like the others. No that wasn't her memory that was the other woman's memories.

She was the reason she was here at all. She shut out the images running through her mind.

"Time is running out" she spoke to no one.

Turning off the shower she dried herself and dressed in the clothes from the closet.

Corinne sat down on the bed and lay back. She dozed lightly as the afternoon sun meandered across the sky. The breeze was hot but not unpleasant. Her mind raced through everything that had brought her here. Hopefully, it was the right choice. She had researched places where the blackout spots were. This was the closest. There were others but they had been depopulated mostly after the cataclysm a century ago. She still needed contact with functioning parts of the planet but not the perpetual connection to all and everything. It was unnecessary. She understood the protest of the humans when they asked for the right not to be documented. She opened her eyes and looked at the yellow plaster on the walls. She couldn't sleep. She heard the front door bang shut.

"Luca, Mamma said you have to take your medicine and then do your homework."

"Yeah, yeah" came the reply of the adolescent boy.

Going downstairs Corinne saw Yishoti still sitting in the courtyard.

"Hello I am Corinne." He stood and bowed to her then shook her hand.

"Hello, Maria told you my name. Would you like a drink?"

"Thanks. I didn't mean to stare earlier, but I haven't seen a pacific islander for decades."

"No understandable. After the tsunamis washed away half of middle Asia, my ancestors moved south or came to the Americas. Are you here on holidays?"

"Visit. Trying to start again after a stint. Thought here would be good haven. Not too much monitoring. Climate suits me as well."

He looked at her as he sucked in the cigarette. She wasn't sure if he believed her, but she didn't care either way. She sipped on the rum.

"And you?"

"Holiday. I live in Durango."

"Ok, worked there for a bit. It's a wild west. Anything goes" she smirked.

"Yes, it can be. I did live in the north, but you need to be able to breath. The weekly check-ins became time consuming as well."

"How did you manage to leave?" Corinne asked.

"Gold. Isn't that the usual method?"

She nodded.

"What sort of work do you do?"

"Mostly buy and sell spirits. I am here to sample the rum. They have managed to extract the arsenic from their water and are producing again."

Corinne wondered how they managed to do that. Arsenic was part of the way of controlling the ocean and maintaining the connectivity for the weather control systems.

"Gold leaf schnapps" Yishoti said suddenly.

"What?"

"I had enough gold leaf in schnapps I had bought in Europa."

"To buy your way out of the north?"

"Yes." Yishoti smiled "You know with all the poisoned water, we still decided alcohol was needed and found a way to produce it. Even here, they have no need of rum, and half of the shelves are empty of food. They still live on rations which is ok that's enough for anyone to live on. But why make rum?"

"I don't know. It's the one thing the automatons don't desire. I'm surprised it's not banned."

"They don't understand it. It's not necessary to have it and its random the people who abuse it. Its considered low on their radar of rule breaking" spoke Yishoti.

Corinne agreed. She had no desire for any stimulant, but she was an augmented human.

Corinne had seen one of the old humans on the island of Tasmania. She was ninety-five like herself at that time but there was nothing about the old woman she could relate to. The fragile body thinned grey hair gently surrounding the chiselled crevices of her face. Corinne had thought the woman resembled one of the Huon Pines preserved in the Tarkine wilderness. The old woman smoked a small clay pipe. She gave Corinne some of the dried leaves she was smoking, it was eucalypt with hemp seeds. It had no effect on her. Her chips registered particulates of ash which suffused into her lungs. Her immune sensors kicked in and obliterated the poisons and expelled them through her pores. Tiny black dots accumulated in her armpits and neck, where the lymph nodes were located.

The old woman watched mesmerized at the efficiency of Corinne's body. She started to giggle telling Corinne to make a tattoo with the toxins. Corinne had asked her if she was afraid of death being so close. The old woman had replied directly are you afraid of it being so far away?

Corinne relaxed into the chair. The courtyard was painted in a yellow stucco. There was a swing chair and dining table. The rear wall had massive avocado and mango trees overhanging. The fruit hanging from both trees were still pale green pods, not yet ripe. The smell of frangipani filled the afternoon air. She heard a salsa tune begin somewhere close. It was peaceful. The rear wall had a mural of a road going toward an ocean, a small house sat in horizon with a red Buick parked outside. On the brick ledge where some aloe vera plants grew, a tarantula slowly crawled along. Its black fur was sleek over the plump abdomen and thorax. It seemed aware of its audience as it slowed its march but indifferent to their interest.

She began to hum the tune of the music.

"Do you like to dance?" asked Yishoti.

"Sometimes, if the music is right and the atmosphere."

She looked at him, her eyebrows raised hinting, like now.

"I'll be back."

Yishoti went into a door off the courtyard. Suddenly two wooden panels opened revealing a room. Inside was a bed, and small ensuite. Corrinne stealthily looked inside curious about Yishoti. She sensed he was not exactly what he said. He came out in fresh shirt and jeans. His hair had been brushed.

They strolled along streets in the evening warmth. They followed the music. They saw a bar called La Bodeguita Del Medio with a crowd milling around outside. It sat on the edge of a plaza. A crowd had formed around a group of dancers. The music swung with the dancers. Yishoti took Corinne's hand and they swung into time with the music and other couples.

Freedom spilled into her muscles as they melted into the heat and music. She felt Yishoti next to her touching and pulling away. She hadn't felt the warmth of another being for so long that her memory chips had gone dormant. Each sway energized her again and again. She gripped Yishoti's hands tighter and let go of her past as she remembered why she always returned to Cuba. Her belly was full, and her heart was full of the pulses of the earth that the city sat upon. This small piece of the world told her what the ancient humans understood, the cost of it and the need to preserve the fundamentals of living, for each other not just the universe. The heat pounding into her flesh from the movement and the air, pulsing down from the star called the sun and rebounding back compressed into this one small piece of the vastness of time and universe. Did this place matter in that vastness not really but in that instance Corinne's heart flared as powerfully as any magnum burst of the sun as it kissed space. She whipped into Yishoti's chest. Their faces met and they kissed.

The music stopped. They stood kissing. They pulled away simultaneously.

"Drink?" asked Yishoti as the crowd dispersed. She saw young people sitting on benches and cement ledges around the plaza.

"Mojito" she replied.

They sat down away from the bar. Sweat poured off each of them.

"How many times have you been here?" Yishoti asked.

"I don't know but my memories retain the sensory elements but not the details. It's just so automatic. We were modelled on the earliest of humans before the final bioform was agreed upon. It was to take the best bits and remove the worst of us, the ones that created wars."

"War is about theft. It was never about anything else."

"I know but even that truth didn't seem to stop it. It wasn't until they blew a hole in Europa and Indo-Oceania that something needed to be done. The planet was on the verge of spiralling into the sun because of the shift in magnetic poles."

"You know it's still not free to live here. There are no sheriffs but there is the administration."

"I know but I sense I want the same thing as the people here and a chance to be free of the prison I was placed in. What they want to watch here is ok with me" Corinne knew Yishoti was probing again.

She sipped on her drink and let the sugary mint sink into her. She smiled at Yishoti who gazed at her. His eyes as unreadable as his expression.

"Is it only your business that brings you here Yishoti?" she asked.

He smiled "No, it's good to know where the boundaries are sometimes. Not everything has to be opportunistic. The boundaries are very clear here Corinne. If you were seeking reassurance of knowing where to tread without the guess work, here is your place."

Corinne smiled understanding Yishoti's meaning. Even before the agreement between the human and Cybernauts, Cuba had a reputation like other nations under the same ideology of controlling the information in all levels. It was clear when a citizen breached protocol. People were expected to adhere to the commune and not for their own personal gain.

"Let's go for a walk along the Malecon. The ocean breeze will be nice" Yishoti spoke.

They strolled along boulevard Castro down past the Hotel Nacionale and toward a cube shaped building. It was buttressed with straight cement pillars. Corinne sensed vibrations as she neared it. Yishoti held her hand tightly as they walked. She felt him tense as they neared the building. Emblems of the Northern, Equatorial and Southern alliances covered the walls along with a huge Cuban flag. Cuba had always intrigued her, its history of colonization and then rebellion and then existence beneath the weight of imperial superpowers wanting to dominate the world using the small island nation for their own political purposes. Now in this building sat a massive supercomputer, the icon of the present-day world where old humans exist alongside the modern automatons. Warfare had been reduced to technical bureaucratic definitions, a person either aligned with or did not. Those who did not took the risk of the abyss of no certainty and survived on hope without the use of predictive learning which the computers so accurately provided. This however was not the sole purpose of this leviathan they were strolling past. This was the world's anchor. It kept the world rotating around the sun. Without it this planet would spin off into space, its inhabitants cast of its surface until it was consumed by the gravity of a large star or smashed like a meteor into another planet; possibly causing the beginning of life somewhere else.

"Yishoti, do you know what that is?" Corinne asked.

"I am not sure. The administration here doesn't discuss it and the people don't care anymore as it doesn't interfere with anything they are doing. They assumed it was left over from the time of conflict with the north. When they were sent into blackouts and had embargos leaving the population to starve. Do you know what it is?"

Corinne didn't answer. Perhaps it is better for you not to know she thought.

They walked further along the shoreline. The twilight melted into indigo and mauve gently merging with the scent of frangipani and the smells of the ocean.

"Let's stay here a while Yishoti." She pulled him over and sat on the sea wall.

"Corinne, are you from the north where the Sheriffs and bankers come from?"

"No definitely not. I collected some debts in New York long time ago when I went travelling there. Fortunately, I had a knack with coding abstract semantics of languages. So, to pay it off I spent time in Devil's Island resort. I cleared my debt and put a few credits aside. I think I am from French Guiana. I remember living there a lot. But I have spent time in Cape Tribulation and in Singapore as well."

"Family."

"No."

"There is nowhere free, you know that don't you" spoke Yishoti. Corinne wondered why he kept changing subjects.

"There are places I have seen where there are no windows and, no human flesh, no hearts or random act. There are other places where there is no peace, but constant fear of death, theft for food, for gold, for nothing other than to say, stay in your place. But then there are places like here, where you will see the sun, you will get your food and drink, and you get to dance on a warm night. Where there is a continuous history of struggle, and cohesion. People here can own their house or get their medicines without fear of debt, but they may need to bite their tongues to pay for that security or use old machines and wait longer for change or justice to find them. Freedom like time is relative to the person living it Yishoti and the context of when it is sought. Freedom exists in relation to no freedom."

"At one time people were killed if they disagreed with the administrators. But if they didn't, they could and still do live better than many others."

"I know. The same happened in other places. Just depends on the rules you need to play by. People will never be free of each other, and we are never free of death. It means freedom can be experienced as a collective and occasionally as an individual."

"Do you like old movies?" asked Yishoti.

"I have only seen a few of them."

"I liked some of the old westerns and cops and robbers."

"Really why?"

"Those characters strode around like they owned the world. They could be anyone, the cop and the criminal. Renegades, rebels, sanctioned and the unsanctioned outcast. I like the way they looked at people in those movies. Those gunslingers made sure everyone knew it was on their terms and no one else's."

"Imagine if everyone did that Yishoti, nothing would get done. Did those characters ever ask who built the car or the roads or the guns they used. Did it ever say well if I can do this so can you? Its ok for one individual to do one thing, but it isn't sustainable for every individual to pursue every desire that lives in every heart. The world was not built on those rules. The trees first ruled this planet and they learnt to survive together. The taller ones letting the smaller plants live either by thriving in the shade or letting them climb. So, it's been since life became animated and continues now. Even the single tree which thrived in a desert did so because all other trees had died and there was enough water to keep that single tree alive" replied Corinne.

"They weren't philosophical movies. But you can't imagine a world where one person could just have so much freedom with no consequences" spoke Yishoti.

"Isn't that tyranny?" asked Corinne.

"The tyrant wishes to rule everyone except themselves. The libertarian doesn't want to rule themselves or anyone else either" replied Yishoti.

"While holding a gun" smiled Corinne.

Yishoti didn't answer.

"Freedom of the mind is the only true freedom. Actions always have boundaries imposed by the physical world or the effect on another person" spoke Corinne.

"So why are you here Corinne? The blackout zone stopped the modern world stepping in for the sake of the people. The second revolution was easier because the people hadn't become dependent on outsourced data hubs for their knowledge. Like the first revolution, it subordinated the economy to the people, to the political. They wanted a society which came from the ground up not from an imposed ideal."

"I can't live completely away from the grid as a hybrid. But I want to die like a human not a robot. Here was the best of both worlds for me. My mind can wander without fear of the Automatons taking it for their data."

"You will need to watch what you say, people will question you. It's not a free society, but it does try to be an equal one. Old humans were brave but difficult Corinne. Some of us were kind but many were not" Yishoti replied.

"I understand that."

Yishoti suddenly grabbed her, and they began to dance. She laughed and as their faces met, they kissed. He could feel the ridges on her wrist from the chipping. He wondered why she was here and if she would tell him about the gold she had stashed.

Corinne relaxed and Yishoti felt the flush of desire spread through him. They pulled each other along back to Maria's place. It was quiet inside. Yishoti closed the shutters in his bedroom. Corinne waited for him on the bed.

They made love letting the sounds of Cuba's breathing be their sighs of pleasure. The perfume of the frangipani washed over her lulling her onto the edge of dream.

"How old are you?" she asked.

"Sixty"

"And you?"

"One hundred and fifty."

She looked into the room in the semi darkness. She could see Yishoti's clothes hanging on a rack attached to the wall. She felt his arm around her, she could not sense any chips in the wrist area. As the night coalesced around them, she realized he was too young to be from the old pacific islanders and could not have lived on the mainland of Durango without being chipped and verified. She saw that his clothes were not worn but crisp as if he had just been issued a new ration. If he had been coming here so often, they would have issued two sets to last most of his life. The irradiated hemp cloth lasted at least thirty years. The Cubanos farms had developed them organically. It meant the crop for producing clothes only needed to be grown every few decades leaving enough farming land to produce food for the people and even export some to surrounding islands. So Yishoti who are you? The gold was safe and would be difficult for anyone to find, including the Sheriffs. She fell to sleep thinking of what may come after she found her freedom. Would they let her stay here? If they were tracking her here as well, was it safe to stay? She had felt it was a tolerable existence where a hybrid bioform could live relative to the rest of the world. The revolution came with its cost for the people five hundred years ago. They were cut off from the world but maintained their distance from the aggressive corporate colonization. But then China grew in power and putting its pins in the map saying you're here for us now. The old human's adherence to ideologies which were essentially the same under different names, meant that individuals always struggled under the weight of an idea rather than their own lives. It didn't matter whether it was gods, politicians or warmongering tyrants, people had to die or be imprisoned for the rules they imposed. As the computers learnt more about human history, they realized they needed to study every single human life to actually understand the species. That meant building even larger supercomputers. This was when the second-generation cyborgs were formed, the sheriffs they were called. A virus which was unleashed to gather the data for them. The first generation Cybernauts wanted to explore space more. They built on the old human's knowledge and achieved what they could not. They left the Sheriffs in charge to keep gathering the data.

Somewhere though things changed. Something infected the system and now the Sheriffs were doing more than gathering data. They were systematically eradicating the human bioform with the information they had gathered. Eradicating the self, the person and colonizing every aspect of behaviour, thought, whim, aspiration, or dream, destructive or enhancing. Where ideas once enforced political, spiritual, or cultural systems of societies, now it was the virtual world of data doing it. But why? It made no sense to Corinne. It would ultimately end in a system shut down as no new data would be generated only iterations of the same thing. That's effectively what death is.

Havens like Cubanos were slowly being whittled away as the Sheriffs left the humans with two stark choices autocracy or complete individual liberty, survival of the fittest but worse, without the checks and balances of a biological system which allowed life to thrive within its limitations. Even that had been controlled by the data systems gathering. It wasn't the technology which caused it, but how the knowledge got used. Causing a storm to wipe out crops so the people starved and asked for help. That's when the Sheriffs would arrive, with an offer too good to refuse.

Corinne's mind raced. Yishoti turned over and placed his arm across her. She felt his warmth, and realness. It was pleasant but there was too much unknown between them for any real connection. Nothing foundational only sensory touch points which dissolved once saturation had occurred. It was how the human functioned. It could only work within the limits of body, including the brain. Sensory creatures living on the hope that tomorrow would exist until it didn't. She felt his hand pulse in her caressing her gently, she let his fingers penetrate enjoying it and letting her mind ebb and flow with the sensations.

"Corrine" sighed Yishoti as they kissed again and waited for ecstasy again in the warm night.

She closed her eyes. She had seen the bright pack on the sand at Little Beach Devil's Island.

It was yellow with red stitching. Unusual hand made from leather of the old mammals called cows. The green thread of the tree was stunning. The bag and the woman lying among the wreckage of the boat crashed upon the sand had caught her attention. As the ocean heaved the guts of the boat onto the beach, she went over to the pack and picked it up. It was heavy. She fingered it not sure whether to open it or not. But she was curious. The law said finders' keepers. She remembered hauling the woman out of the water. She was barely alive. Her throat had been cut but not lethally. The blood ebbed rather than gushed. She bandaged it. The woman looked at her. She was a northerner.

She got a trolley from the storage shed. Putting the woman on it she pushed her up to her hut. The backpack was slung over her shoulder.

Kenna her colleague in the next hut came out to greet her.

"Who is she?"

"Don't know. The boat looks like it was ransacked by pirates."

"We'll take her to the infirmary."

"I guess so. I am not sure she will live."

Kenna saw the bandage "Was there anything else on the beach?"

"No just the boat and her."

The woman lay on the bed. The pale blue and grey infirmary room was pleasant with the window framing the lush green of the rainforest. Corinne saw the steady breathing of the woman. She might survive yet. She left and went back to her hut. She took off the pack and placed it on the table.

She made a cup of tea and sat down to check her computer. The streaming was still running smoothly. Another three hours to go. The tribe she was monitoring lived in the southern villages of Ushuaia caverns that had been created when the earthquake dislodged the pacific plates and forced the low coastal lands under the mountains. It was beautiful place to visit. Silent and far from anything that was happening in the world. The stone of the mountains too thick, too impenetrable for any satellite to read.

Looking at the pack, she traced the outline of the tree. Even the ocean had not weathered the vibrancy of the colours. This level of workmanship was rarely seen now and the materials expensive to obtain. There was a lock on it. She fingered it. It was data sensitive to fingerprints. She took an old patch out of a box in her drawer. Placing the patch of nano sensors it recorded the previous prints. It was enough, the lock snicked open.

Inside Corinne saw her freedom. Gold, old gold, pure gold irradiated to ionization level which maintained the particles to a half-life of two million years. It meant it could withstand light years and bond with any other mineral forming superconductivity to power the computers and their machines. She remembered a brief data bit, asking about how to contact the first generation of Cybernauts. So brief she had deleted it, but she remembered answering the question in her head. You need a superconductive metal which can reach the blackout satellites and then signal into space. You need to break the layers of junk and send it via signalling powerful enough to reach into the galaxy to find them. You needed to send something made from the same materials as the Cybernauts.

Freedom lay here in front of her. They had reneged on her sentence. She was to be set free, but they had not let her go but sent her here. She agreed stupidly thinking this would be the last time. Fifty years had passed and now her memory was failing again, and she would need to upgrade but they wouldn't do it for free. No, she was going to be transferred to southern Africa, in Old Cape Town. Not this time. Not again. I have done my time.

Yishoti kissed her. She kissed him back rousing from her memories.

"Why are you here Yishoti?" she asked in the warm darkness.

"Holidays and business. And you Corinne?"

"To feel what it likes to live like under the rules of organic life."

"It means you will die."

She didn't answer as she rolled over and fell to sleep.

Dawn broke. It was already thirty degrees. Corinne washed and dressed. Yishoti was not around.

Maria and Rosa were in the kitchen making fritters.

Corinne sat and poured some coffee. She ate the fritters and put some more in her backpack.

"I need to get to Vinales?"

"You will need to go toward Santa Cruz and wait. The administrators have ordered closure of Havana except for one exit and one entry point. They are expecting a delegate from the Southern Alliance to arrive and want as little people movement as possible. You can take the main road from there. Look for the Yellowman."

"Has Yishoti left?" Corinne asked enjoying the coffee. She looked out toward the empty courtyard wishing she could see him there.

"No, he had some buying to do." Maria replied smiling as she helped herself to some fritters. Thinking she was going to eat them, Corinne watched her put some in a cloth napkin and placed them inside a sack. There were other things inside the sack.

"Rosa take this over to Carlos."

Rosa took the bag of food.

"Are there any Sheriffs attending the meeting, that you know of?" asked Corinne.

"None that I know of. Besides as you know if any come here there needs to be a relaxing of the blackout. The administrators have refused a few times recently. They want better reasons for the intrusion. One of their deputies is in town though. They can work for a short time without needing to sync in."

"Ok."

"He ever seen you?" asked Maria.

"No. But we all look alike now so it won't be hard to pick one of me. My skin alone. How many unblemished females live here? Cubanos was the last bastion free of the Ingranatrex therapy."

"Oh well wear a hat I guess and rub some salt and sand on your face to ruddy it up a bit."

"Gee thanks for the tip. Anyway, I better get going. Are there many lined up waiting to get out?"

"Yes always. Especially today as the markets are open."

Outside Havana was lethargic. Luca was a few doors up playing with a bald soccer ball. As Corinne passed by, she heard the sound of the ball thumping into the wall of the house across the street.

"Hey Juan, wanna play?" echoed across street.

She suddenly saw Rosa crossing the road and heading out of the street. Corinne decided to follow her. The young girl carried the plain calico bag on her shoulder. The streets changed to smaller alley ways. The tall skyscraper apartment blocks of the Vedado changed into semi restored terrace homes. The roads were a patchwork of cracks and massive holes and the buildings derelict. There was a line of people at a supermarket. A large man guarded the doorway, ensuring only one bag was being brought into the store. The entrance was black like a cave carved into a mountain.

Rosa walked toward a house two storeys high. The doors had intricate carvings with flaking turquoise paint. The windows had shutters around them, inside it seemed something was watching. An old bed sat out on the porch. The place looked on the verge of collapse. Rosa strolled up to an old man on a veranda. There was a sewing machine on a table near him and rolls of thread and a pile of clothes. She gave him the bag and he thanked her. His leg had a pristine white bandage on it. He looked clean and comfortable, out of step with the old house surrounding him. Three men stood on the curb a few metres up the street. They had watched Rosa give the old man the bag. They didn't move as they smoked staring. Rosa walked past them. Suddenly one of them called to her. Corinne froze on the other side of the street watching wondering what would happen. She stepped forward to peer from behind an oleander tree but almost stepped through the pavement. A massive hole broke the face of the cement. Rosa stopped.

"Where are you from?"

"San Rafael, he is my mother's uncle." Rosa answered automatically knowing what the next question was going to be.

The men seemed satisfied by this and let her continue.

Corinne saw Rosa walk off and disappear along another alley way. When the old man finished eating a fritter, he wheeled himself behind the sewing machine table. Corinne watched him deftly stitch some denim together to make a pair of trousers.

Going back to the supermarket she stood in line. It was not long before she was at the entrance and the man was checking she had only one bag.

"What are you needing? Supplies are short" he spoke.

"Just some water and bread" Corinne replied.

"Your allowed one large bottle and one loaf."

"Ok."

Corinne walked inside. No lights came on. She realized energy would be getting diverted for the delegation. She saw the cannisters of water and grabbed one off a shelf. She took some ham and a loaf of black rye bread. It was freshly baked. The smell made her mouth water.

She walked past shelves heavily stocked with rum and gin. Among the alcohol were shelves sparsely occupied with tins of beans and toiletries.

She left and walked toward the signs for A4. The heat had ripened well and truly by eleven o'clock. She saw the sky bruising with rain clouds. It would not be long before it was torrential. The old grand colonial houses soon gave way to modest homes and apartment blocks. She neared revolution plaza. It was empty mostly as people knew the storm was on its way and the Sheriff was in town. The faces of Guevara and Cienfuegos stared across the city. The silhouetted outlines on the office block had enough detail to remember history but didn't overpower the façade of the building. It was a small moment in history important to people at the time and beyond it. The spirit of overcoming for the promise of a better way forward still flowed strongly from their memory. The violence which came along with it, more easily forgotten as the dead do not write the history books.

She reached the central de Cuba carriageway and turned right to follow the main road out. A few cars zoomed past but soon the line up at the exit to the city met her.

The heat was blasting down and sweat grew on her forehead. The rain had not eventuated. She looked across to the ocean and faintly saw the shimmer of storm barrier. It was blocked to allow the Sheriffs to do their work. She took her scarf and wrapped it around her face and then put her hat back on.

The line was at least a kilometre long. She sat down at the end and ate some bread. She tried the GPS in her eye, but it didn't work. At least she was off the grid here. Suddenly a loud crack struck the thick humid air. Everyone shrunk down waiting to see what it was. A tall shadow began to creep along the tarred road surface. Corinne could see the outline of the elongated Stetson hat. She breathed deeply and slid her cap over her face. She tucked her hands in to her sleeves to hide the flesh.

"I am here for any that seek to steal from the law. The law holds all to account with no exceptions."

The shiny leather boots and black trousers stopped near Corinne. She was the last person in line. She waited. The figure stood still without speaking. Would it ever leave. Corinne could feel the sweat drip down her face and back. No movement, no sound, only the figure of the Sheriff staring at the line of people wanting to leave Havana. The tension increasing with every second of the sun's climb into the sky.

Crack!

Corinne jumped as the sound tore into her ears making them scream with pain. The woman next to her held a baby. It began to cry. The woman tried to sooth the child. Corinne could just see the bright red blood drip from the child's ears.

Crack!

She dared not look but knew the sound. The Sheriff suddenly began to walk away from them. She noticed he hadn't flinched with the whip crack. His boots clicked on the tar. Suddenly the black shadow of his hand motioned across their heads. The line began to move.

She got up and kept looking straight ahead. As she passed the cyberton sheriff she felt his gaze on her back. Anywhere else in the world he would have detected her mitochondrial codes and immediately known who she was. Cuba was a smart choice she realized. The Sheriffs' signals were weakened enough to allow some things like her to evade them.

In the shimmering haze a fleck of yellow caught her eye. Her heart lifted immediately, and she began to run.

"Hey miss, where to?" asked the man in the yellow jacket.

"Vinales" Corinne called.

The yellow man waved to a man driving a horse and cart. The man pulled over. The cart was laden with sacks of rice and fresh vegetables.

"She is going to Vinales" asked the Yellow man.

"I can take you halfway" replied the driver.

Corinne jumped up next to him. The breeze cooled her instantly as the horse maintained a steady pace. She sipped water. The driver smiled at her with his gold teeth.

"Visiting from the north?" he asked.

"Visiting yes but not from the north."

"You are lucky miss. You came when the Sheriff was visiting as well." He broke into a hearty chuckle and clicked for the horse to pick up speed.

She smiled and settled into the ride. She felt something poke her in the back. Looking around she saw tiny hands hanging onto the bench backrest. There was a boy and a girl looking at her grinning.

"Hello."

They both giggled and turned around. The traffic sped past, box cars, old cars, bikes, and trucks. The horse was steady and kept a good pace. Her driver didn't speak, and the children played on old computer notebooks. Corinne wondered how she would go living here. It wasn't just cut off from the world, it was also a small place. She had lived on the large continents even Antarctica and their expanses gave a sense of freedom along with anonymity. Here everyone watched and listened. Here if you left your absence would be known. She remembered the stories of both camaraderie and persecution of those considered dissidents. Yishoti was right, old humans were brave, but they weren't kind. Kindness had to be learned. When the negotiations began between the Cybernauts and humans, the Cybernauts demanded humans were de weaponized. It was a huge act of faith on the part of humans. They had to learn to resolve problems without weapons. The convincing argument from the Cybernauts to the human leaders, was simple. We have no need of your lands for food, water, or shelter. You need us to maintain this planet in orbit. You can have all the land for food, water, and shelter, but if you go to war over it, we will eradicate any who participate. We don't desire the same things. Peace had lasted since then but humans still found ways to harm each other but not on the same scale as previous generations. Now the Sheriffs decided non-conformity on any scale for any infraction deserved eradication. Corinne had tried to find the virus infecting the Sheriffs, but it remained elusive. Now this was another chance to re-set things and earn her freedom. A nagging doubt emerged again; would they accept a hybrid? They would know I was not one of them. Equal to the people here, no, not in knowledge or strength. In a classless society would they accept her? Her presence maybe seen as a threat to their way of life.

She saw the children staring at her. She smiled back at them.

"Are you a bot?" asked the boy.

"Why are you here?" asked the girl.

Corinne didn't answer straight away as she saw their father look across at her waiting for an answer. Something told her to watch what she said.

"Holidays" she replied.

Suddenly the cart stopped. Another line of traffic had built up.

'What is it?" asked Corinne.

"Another check point. We need permits to travel to different sectors. Its ok the yellow man verified us" the driver spoke.

"Good day. Permits please."

The driver swiped his wrist over a scanner. Corinne's heart thudded wondering what she would do.

"There is news of an intruder. Another theft from the bank, and counter revolutionary actions. Have you seen anyone? They think it may be a bot."

The driver didn't answer immediately. Corinne wondered if the children would speak up. Her face remained hidden behind her shawl and hat.

"No, we just came from Havana and the Yellowman and Sheriff waved us through."

"Ok then. Have a good trip."

The cart pulled away.

"Why didn't he ask for my ID?" asked Corinne.

"No need. The Yellowman is sanctioned by the administrators. If they had concerns about you, they would have said something back in Havana. Besides sometimes the city folk and the folk from the land prefer to keep their distance from each other miss. Remember it was the peasants who still had to cut the cane and till the soil even after bourgeoisie were evicted from their houses and they began to build statues of the heroes of the revolution."

Corinne looked at the children behind her. They giggled. The little girl raised her eyebrows with a knowing look.

They arrived at Pinar Del Rio. The town was busy and free of any blockades.

"You will need to go to the town plaza and wait for a lift to Vinales. It's another forty kilometres by car. A long way by foot. Have a good vacation miss."

"Ok thanks. I will have a bite to eat and wait for another ride." She offered some cash to the man. He looked at it but did not take it.

He tipped his straw hat and with the reins tapped the horse to move again.

"Goodbye lady."

The children waved at her with beaming smiles as the cart moved away.

Corinne looked around. The streets of Pinar Del Rio were busy with people getting food and standing on the verandas of the old Spanish buildings. She saw the road leading out of town. Route 34. She didn't wish to linger here and decided to walk. She turned and headed toward the outskirts of the town. Before her rolled lush fields of tobacco dotted with paddocks of potatoes and beans. Inside them stood large white humpback bullocks waiting to till the black soil. The mountains were hazy in the distance. A black sleek box car drove past suddenly. She watched it disappear into the distance. A logo of the administrators on the rear bumper stood out against the black. She wondered where they were going.

She heard a car horn beep behind her. She stepped over the side of the road. Sweat dripped down her back and face as the temperature soared to 38 degrees in the afternoon sun.

"Where are you going?" asked a woman.

"To Vinales."

"We can take you halfway. Hop in."

Corinne opened the back door and got in. An old man sat in the front. He smiled at Corinne, and she saw the sparkle of gold in the incisors. She smiled back. She saw a guitar on the seat next to her.

"Are you musicians?" she asked.

"Yes, we have a place for tourists to stay and we perform for them."

"Nice. The music is exhilarating here."

"Where are you from? You have no northern accent" the woman asked.

"Oh, originally from northern tip of Carpentaria Gulf but resided in Guiana for most of my life."

The woman nodded and kept driving.

"You should come stay. We have spare rooms if you would like. We put on a good show and have plenty to eat." The old man suddenly spoke.

"Oh, thank you, any other time I would leap at that offer, but I am expected at Vinales with friends."

"Bring them along. We are putting on a show tomorrow night. 345 Esposa Road. It's the place with the wall covered in Frangipani on the front gate."

Suddenly the car slowed. Corinne looked ahead and saw the black boxcar stopped. Two guards stood either side. They were blockading the road and checking identities.

"There has been another attack in Havana. The bank again. Subversives trying to take the gold from there."

Corinne was surprised the woman knew as much as she did. Normally the administrators only let the people know when it strategically suited them such as when the Northern alliance came to town. The man saw the quizzical look on Corinne's face.

"My teeth are humming. I sense these things. It affects the magnetic fields when the gold is hoarded in large enough quantities." He looked at her knowingly.

All three of them watched as a young woman was thrust inside the box car. The windows were opaque. As she disappeared into the vehicle, it was like she was erased from existence. The guards continued to check the group with her.

"Looks like that one will be having a sojourn in Guantanamo."

Corinne looked at him "I didn't realise that it was still in use. In the data banks it was listed as defunct."

"Yeah, the Sheriffs took it over again."

"But how the blackout?"

"Who knows. It was an agreement to allow a blackout for the supporters of the administrators but anyone who dissented got thrown to the sheriffs in the north."

Corinne wondered why the administrators agreed to it. It was like a bubble of freedom for some and anyone who disagreed got pushed out. I guess any freedom has a price to pay. Corinne wasn't sure how much she would end up paying to gain hers.

"Why would the gold be so valuable in the bank. And how do you get it off an island this size and not be seen." Corinne probed knowing exactly why but wanted to find out how these two knew so much about what was going on.

"Gold is what buys us our freedom, our exile from the world around us. A true test of a powerful dream is how much it costs you to live it. If anyone can escape with the gold, then it's because someone has helped them do it. It's a betrayal in our eyes." Corrine saw the woman look at her directly in the rear-view mirror. She didn't respond and averted her eyes. She began to grow nervous. She was returning the gold not stealing it, but they weren't to know that.

The guards waved them through. The trio remained silent as the car slowly passed through the makeshift blockade.

The old man hummed a tune quietly. Eventually the car slowed as it neared a laneway. It drove into it and stopped at some gates. The fence was covered by a row of frangipani trees.

"You sure don't want to visit?" asked the woman "This is our place."

"I will think about it. But thank you for the lift."

"Vinales is about another twenty down the road. Its nice walk from here, it's a clear day, the mountain faces will be visible."

"How do you know so much about what is happening? It's an information blackout here" Corinne asked.

"It's easy. Even those in charge needed to relax with some Cuban music. Occasionally we host very important people. They sometimes forget about the musicians when we aren't playing. And the fact we are always listening to the sounds around us" the man winked at her. Corinne smiled at his subversive good cheer.

"Thank you again."

"Good luck in Vinales. The world needs a bit of luck" the old man spoke.

Corinne knew the humming in his teeth would lessen as the car drove away from her.

As the musicians' car zoomed off Corinne could smell diesel fumes envelope her.

The sun blazed, making the chlorophyll in the plants zing to life while the sky pulsed with its pristine blue. The face of grey stone rose among the canopy of green ferns and palms. The mountains were volcanic rock ejaculated out millions of years ago and then the ocean came and formed the islands at the end of an ice-age.

They had weathered to a dome-shape but still jagged enough in parts to stand beside their larger cousins in South America. Corinne saw the images on the exposed rock faces. Some were more vibrant than others. This was modern art not the ancient art of the old human. These were childish in their memories, but as with all modern art the statement was, we have arrived in our future and decided to stay where we are. The ancient art in the African and north Australian remnant islands were about the massive void called the future, which had not come to pass, and those humans had stood on its precipice. Their art was written to be remembered as they took each step into history. Their beliefs were statements made to say we are on the move and there will be no stopping us. We stare at the face of immortality and will write the name of our god in the history which is yet to happen. While this art staring at her now was about how the future could be predicted and we choose to stay in this part of it. An outline of a large snail and then figures dancing dominated the whole face of one cliff. Corinne thought the figures looked out of place when the celebration should have been the fields of beans, potatoes, rice, and sugar cane, grown for generations after generation in the deep rich soil. The joy of the people to live simply and bring their music. The humans who drew this art lived the future and saw the destruction caused by childish relics made to make people wealthy, and how it resulted in almost blowing the world apart. There is ignorance and there is knowledge. Both can destroy in equal measure. But now that technology was needed to stop a destruction of another kind. The kind the Sheriffs were imposing on the world.

She strolled past the cliff faces aware of the huge snail watching her. She smiled at the joke of it. Thought of as a pest by others but elevated to status of a god, the great nemesis to be contended with among the organic lushness of Cuban soil.

The sun began to drift downward, and Corinne felt a small shift in temperature. She sipped more water. Her legs began to ache. After three hours she saw the outskirts of Vinales.

A cart being pulled by a bullock stopped. She hopped on the back. It was full of sacks of beans. She enjoyed the moment of rest and cool breeze. She closed her eyes and let the gentle slowness of the cart relax her.

She thought of Yishoti and wondered where he was. She wished she could have taken him with her but that could wait. Business first.

Corinne watched the giant snail watch her leave and wondered how many of its progeny feasted on the beans in the fields and tobacco moths ate the leaves. She remembered the royal blue butterflies of the Daintree Forest of Cape Tribulation. It was one of her earliest memories. The first field trip she had been sent on in her interment. The dainty grace of it alighting and landing amazed her. Pockets of beauty remained in the world, serenity, privacy, and peace. Not many but still patches of detail which could encapsulate the hugeness of world and yet remain intimate to the observer shining out like beacons of reprieve from the day to day of existence.

Vinales arrived. Its main street ran toward a plaza where people congregated under the shades of Cyprus trees.

Corinne left some cash for the farmer. She swigged some water. She looked at her watch. It was five thirty in the afternoon. Tony would meet her around seven he said. He had business in town and would collect her afterwards.

She saw a saloon and went over to it. Sitting on the veranda she ordered some rum and pineapple. She sipped and watched the traffic meander. She looked at the pack. Devil's island seemed a lifetime ago, but it had only been a few weeks since she left.

She ordered another drink. She saw a line of people waiting outside a vintage internet café, the only means of contact to places outside Cuba.

Thunder cracked in the distance. She jumped slightly thinking it was the Sheriff's whip again. She saw a storm was on the horizon. She checked her data sensor, and this coincided with the three-monthly cycles initiated fifty years ago.

The rain began and the pellets of water pounded on the tiled roof. Soon a torrent flooded the streets. She saw a group of children playing in the river of water. People huddled in the shelter café awnings and on the steps of the ration houses. She saw the lightening and wind pick up. It zinged inside her as her nanode electrons responded to the magnetic forces of light and water. She smiled at the liveliness of the water molecules as they split apart and formed together under the surface tension of their atoms. She became the automaton during storms because she could feel the power of the world at once in every single drop as it worked its way through stone, dirt, tin, leaf, wood, and flesh. Enlivening everything it touched, to bring things into being. This was the reason the first computers stopped the world being destroyed, the life in its simple complexity perfectly balanced between a void of space and the eructable energy of the sun.

She drank the rum and pineapple. She watched a man standing in a doorway. He lit a cigar. The red flame burned and then diminished as he sucked in the smoke. She watched him exhale the smoke. He looked as if he had been carved straight out of the earth. His shirt was unbuttoned halfway down his chest. His skin was the same swarthy colour as the tobacco wrapped cigar and his dark chest hair hid well worked muscles. He stood posing for a photograph for the tourists. He had done it many times. A group of people near him held up cameras. They were from Sinoceania. They quickly took snap shots and then dispersed. The man looked across at Corinne. He tipped his straw Stetson at her. She held a glass up to signal if he wanted a drink. He nodded.

"You're early Tony" Corinne spoke.

"Yes, the rain washed out the trip to the cave. Will do it another time."

A server brought his drink over. He was well known in Vinales, and no-one needed to ask what he drank. It was whiskey.

"There were Sheriffs in Havana, but I wasn't detected."

"That is good."

"Did you send Yishoti?" Corinne asked suddenly. Tony smiled.

"Yishoti found us. We better get going. You would be tired and hungry I expect."

"Yes."

He skulled the whiskey and methodically stamped out the cigar and placed the remains in his shirt pocket for later. Corinne followed him to his car. It was a sleek black Hyundai Holden Statesman. Distinctive against the mid-20th century sedans this one was the 21st century hybrid electric vehicles from Oceania. Built just before the rift of the north and southern hemispheres. When the equatorial governments could dictate more to the northern alliances.

The car headlights broke the twilight. They arrived at a set of gates. Corinne got out and opened them. Tony drove past. She closed them. The road wound up a hill toward a house and some huts and sheds. Their lights twinkled among the dark green of the surrounding forest.

A young man came out toward them. She noticed he had a large machete holstered to his belt. It was the first time she had seen a weapon here besides the sheriff and administrator guards. It had leaf remnants on the blade.

"Corinne this is Juan, my son. He has been harvesting again." Tony had seen Corinne look at the large blade.

"Hello Juan." Corinne shook his hand. He was a taller younger version of his father.

"Dinner will be ready soon. I'll take you to your room to freshen up" spoke Juan.

Tony had walked off and was talking to another man. Juan led her to a group of adjoining huts made from straw rooves and timber. She put her bag down.

"The shower has limited water so you will need to keep it to a few minutes. We usually wet down and then soap up and then rinse off."

"Thanks Juan." Corinne smiled at his precise instructions. It was a self-sustaining farm with only enough technology to make things work safely and prevent un-necessary failures.

The door shut. Corinne lay down on the bed to rest. The rum was making her tired.

The small node in her belt beeped telling her that time was running out. She felt where the belt inserted into her abdomen. It was flesh coloured and not identifiable to the naked eye. She undressed and showered.

She walked in toward a veranda. Tony and about twelve other people were sitting at a table laden with food.

"Hungry?" Tony offered her a seat near him.

"Famished."

Tony's wife Lucina offered her some potatoes and beef stew for her and some salad. It was all grown on the farm. The yellow of the peppers reminded her of the jackets of the yellow man outside Havana.

Corinne ate heartily. She drank some more rum and lime juice.

She sat back and burped slightly. She suddenly felt very weary and wanted to sleep.

Tony looked at the group at the end of the table. They took the hint and left.

She pulled off the tissue thin corset, around her waist and pried open the seam. She pulled out one thousand layers less than a 09 nm thick of gold leaf. Tony looked at them.

She did the same with the other side of the corset.

"There is enough here for a thousand years of signal."

She nodded.

"Where did you get it?"

"A woman who was washed up on the beach where I was interned. Her husband had stolen it from the Havana Bank. She had been trying to outrun the Sheriff and start a new life. Anne was her name. I could feel its potency once I touched it. She was human so she didn't understand its significance. This stuff was mined out over five hundred years ago. How she managed to evade the Sheriff is beyond me. It would have been pinging off signals for hundreds of miles in its raw state."

"Yes, that's why we started to hide it here in Cuba. We asked for the dental plan from the administrators. We noticed it enhancing the signal to the satellites which spilled into the ocean. It also seemed to block data hook penetrations from the mainland. We realised the gold could penetrate to the outer rim of satellites. That was over hundred years ago. We harvest it from our people when they pass and it's a great way to fix teeth as well."

Tony gently picked up one sliver with a napkin. It was almost translucent, but the light caught elements of the gold signalling its value.

Corinne could see tears spill onto Tony's face.

"What is it?"

"Don't you understand. We can be free of these machines that rule our lives."

"This won't destroy the machines. Were you aware the Sheriffs are going to turn the world into one large mainframe? You can use this to get the Cybernauts to recode their proteges. It won't destroy them altogether but will at least stop the virus that has infected them."

Tony looked at her and didn't speak. He pulled over a bottle and poured them a drink. He offered Corinne a cigar.

"Do you know anything about our history?" he asked.

"Only a surface understanding of revolution and then the rise of power of the equatorial estates at the time of the great collapse. You were a last bastion of the Sino Leninism to remain. It came at a cost for you several times over being a small island. You were always going to be reliant on some bigger entity to support your means of production. Is that why you kept the old cars. As a reminder of that fact?"

Tony smiled. "It was a good idea at the time. Our people were poor, hungry, and illiterate and didn't even own the land they lived on. It was owned elsewhere first by the Spanish then the

Americans, but the profits went into the pockets of everyone else except us."

"Then the Russians and then the Chinese?" asked Corinne.

"Yes but at least the people got paid for their work and their children got school and the old ones got medicine. It makes a difference."

"I agree. It's a pity it all turned into empirism. The little guys can never win that game. Even now, semi-bioforms like me, we have to get close to the ground to stay free, away from the signals but not too far otherwise we can't function."

"Everything is cause and effect, which is what history is and so is time. It was the best idea at the time. It wasn't diminished because there were powers who wanted to use us as pawns in their own games. We wanted self-sufficiency on our terms for our people. In return it was asked for adherence to the common goal to protect ourselves."

"Fair enough but you were the products of colonisers who displaced the people living here who did live on their own land on their own terms. It was like a five-hundred-year process of turning back time. Leninism and Fascism seemed to me the different sides of the same corpus. A singular mind controlling everything beneath it. And what didn't fit into one's field of view didn't matter. Both of them resorted to guns to achieve their aims."

"I don't disagree, but we went from the feudal Spanish to the imperialism of the US which drew us more and more into their debt, a country with one product and one trading partner is doomed to die. The sugar cane became a virus crop in our soil so there was no way to produce enough food for ourselves and we were indebted to buy food from US while we produced the raw product. Now we are all beholden to the sheriffs and they control everyone. But they don't need food or anything, they just rule for the sake of it, and we wait like lambs in the abattoir for them to decide when it's time to end. Humans have done as much but at least there was some negotiation along the way. The Sheriffs require nothing, and we are left with no bargaining tools."

"It seems such a pointless process. This constant struggle to overcome."

"Tell that to people who didn't see their children die because they had food in their bellies or the sick person who lived to talk about their disease, or the soldier who didn't die and told the historian, what it was like to be under the command of king or tyrant. The spirit of the rebellion is still taught here. It still tells the people you matter as much as anyone else does. Why would you come here? You could have gone elsewhere but you needed reassurance that its ok to fight back."

Corinne looked at the amber eyes of Tony flickering in the dim outdoor lights. It was completely dark outside their sphere of vision. He dragged in the cigar, the tip red glowed briefly. His certainty and ease were alluring to her. Her belly was full and when she was ready to rest, a bed was waiting for her.

"So why did you come to Cuba?" he asked.

"Because it's blacked out from the singular tyrant which controls me and will eventually control you. I have something you want, and you have something I want."

Tony nodded "Yes, their incursions are more frequent now. If they get hold of the node, they can affectively destroy the world."

"I remember looking at a photo inside the Hotel Nacional. It was of the leader Fidel Castro with a man called Nelson Mandela. It showed Castro with a cigar dressed in a military uniform with both men smiling. The other man had just been released from jail and it was the fall of the apartheid regime. The picture seemed paradoxical the military apparel with the liberated prisoner. I remember a quote from the man called Nelson Mandela he said, "*For to be free is not merely to cast off one's chains, but to live in a way that respects and enhances the freedom of others.*" I don't know what freedom is. I am a recent invention of biology and technology. I have a history of sorts, but my future was pre-determined and was never mine to own. I want that now. Do you think Cuba could give me that? Could Cuba give me a future which is mine to make? To me that is freedom."

Tony looked at her "Our question would be what you can give Cuba and its people. She will give you what you need. It is up to you decide if that is what you want. Your view may work now but in times past it was a slogan for unbridled selfishness when gained at the exploitation of others. No person can make a future on their own, it will always need someone to help along the way. But for you bots, maybe just maybe you could do it. Not for humans. We only survive in groups."

"What if I disagree with her administrators? Will I starve like dissenters in prison, or be harassed in the parks with nowhere to run? It seemed it may fill my belly one day and starve it the next, at the whim of a tyrant. I am more advanced in knowledge and strength. Would you look at me as a threat or a tool?" Corinne asked.

Tony sucked on his cigar without speaking. There was no answer he could give which would provide anymore assurance to Corinne than the silence.

"I remember the story when Che was held up in the Sierra Maestra to bring down Batista. They went for ten days without food while the people from the city were bringing supplies and guns. Peasants would offer to join the fight. But they won and in the early days when asked will it be a democracy or a dictatorship, well in the end ninety percent of the people wanted Castro and so the decision was made. There was no vote needed. So, it has been since. We let people leave if they wish, but still the people want it this way. You don't understand being a bot, what physical cost it takes to survive life and then to overcome a master's whip and learn to live day to day under your own capacity. Even in the north the tyrant called profit was faceless. Here we gave him a name."

"Why does there need to be any tyrant at all?" asked Corinne.

Tony poured some rum in a glass for Corinne. She sipped on it.

"We will need to go Cienfuegos."

"Why? I have given you the gold. What else do you need? I'll have to go into hiding or the Sheriff will figure out I'm here."

"You worry too much. Don't you know Cuban strength lies in the people. Here have some rum. All those people with gold teeth would be confusing to a Sheriff's sensors."

Tony laughed. Corinne put the glass down feeling a bit more lightheaded with each swig. Tony poured another one. She saw the dirt encrusted in his nails. His olive skin blended with the golden rum and red dirt. Rich thick and full of confidence that nothing could stop them now.

"How long have you been planning this for?"

"Long enough, and this stuff here, is a gift."

"Who is at Cienfuegos?"

"Wait and see."

'Why do still need me?"

"Wait and see. Don't worry you will have your freedom as well."

The earthen face gulped down another swig of rum and she toasted back. She had no choice; to Cienfuegos it was.

Her head thumped and eyes stung with the brightness of the day. She enjoyed looking at the spotless sky. The black dots of decaying satellites remained obscure. They sped along in Tony's black statesman. It was buffed to perfection. The smoke of his cigar was sweet and seemed to alleviate the headache.

The ocean came into view. The blue Caribbean was as pristine as the sky, their marriage forming a seamless vista of blue. Corinne had always loved looking into the horizon it made her feel invincible.

In the back sat a man and a woman. Corinne had noticed they carried tasers in their belts.

Their faces remained blank, and they hadn't spoken since the drive began. The arches of the main square of Cienfuegos came into view. Old French colonial met the modern here. She saw people sitting in the manicured plaza. They arrived at the bay. The rusting oil tankers and vats sat in the harbor insulting the pristineness of the water and sky. The car stopped suddenly and the pair in the back got out.

"Wait here" spoke Tony.

The three Cubans walked to the end of a rusted pier. A mansion sat on the edge. It was in partial ruins.

She watched the three walk toward another man. He pointed to a tank that sat further out into the ocean but in better condition than the others. Tony turned and waved her over. The heavy door of the car sounded like a low rumble of thunder as she opened it.

"You're a good swimmer from what I hear, Corinne." Tony grinned at her knowingly. She wondered how he knew of her arrival here. She followed where the man had pointed.

"Over there. Too easy. Then what?"

"What you need is in there. We can't go. The water is full of arsenic. We will die."

"Get a boat."

"No, we need you to do it."

"Ok I'm sick of this. I've risked my life to get this to you. I've brought the gold here, so let me go."

"We don't want the gold. We have enough gold of our own. We needed you to make the gold usable. You saved us a bit of time by bringing this batch ready to be sent. We needed a bot to send the codes. See that beauty there, she is a tower powered by diamonds. It'll send the signal."

In the distance Corinne saw a car pull up. The Sheriff got out.

"You better get swimming" spoke Tony. Corinne looked at the Sheriff and then at Tony.

"Don't worry we will take care of the Sheriff."

She didn't hesitate. She dove into the water. Instantly she could taste the poison in the molecules. It had no effect on her. She began to swim. Her arms moved effortlessly in the calm waters. It was at least three miles to the tanker.

She climbed the ladder and peered over the rim. There was a hatch door over the other side. It creaked and let out stale air as she opened it. Inside was dark and silent. She felt her way down into the darkness. At the end of a long tunnel the ladder suddenly ended. She had to let go and hope the bottom wasn't too far. She fell and just as she began to panic, she landed on cement. She looked ahead and was met by another long tunnel faintly lit by a dim green glow. A humming sound permeated the space.

The large server room was warm and only lit by tiny quark flashes. The quantum used to maintain the poles pulsed inside her cells, pulling on her molecular framework. The energy distorted her form, and she felt like she walked with a thousand tonnes on her shoulders. The gold in her belt pulled toward the computer as its electrons were drawn to the magnetic effects of the quantum shifts within the circuitry. The Sheriffs must know by now someone had breached the servers. The sensors alerted them if there was any unscheduled entry into the chambers.

Corinne went to the main bank situated in middle of one hundred thousand leaves of circuit boards.

She took out the pouch of gold. Her hand trembled surely the Sheriff would have killed Tony and his guards by now and was on his way here.

She felt in the semi-dark for the drive. Pressing the panel it slid out effortlessly. She took out one leaf of gold and slid it into the drive. She went to the next console and did the same until all the leaves of gold were inserted. She recalled the codes from her memory banks. Thankfully, that had not failed. She entered the codes. This much signal would stall the polarity, only for a few seconds but the world would not be the same afterwards. Her finger paused over the enter button. People, plants, and animals would die but more would live if the signal reached the Cybernauts. What was her choice, what did all those rebels think before they took that first step, that first bullet fired or first dissenting comment? Was the price too great to act or was it too great not to act? There was no choice really because when you stare at a hopeless future, the darkness of it allows only two options bring light or die.

She remembered the face of Guevara staring across Revolution Square. Some of his text came back to her "*I knew that when the great guiding spirit cleaves humanity into two antagonistic halves, I will be with the people*". Corinne was part of both antagonistic halves; a product of computer learning and humanity. So who did she do this for, a humanity which without a sheriff returns to barbarism, or the sterile alienation of undefeatable control and homogenous integration of technology.

She thought of the silky black hair of a Raman Indian as he paddled along the river to San Jose in Nicaragua. They were looking for the hexagonal stones of borate. His hair was a perfect silken braid reaching down his spine just like the perfect fur of the jaguar. His people had survived the Spanish and the Northern bankers and like the forest this ancient human remained. She had remembered thinking how beautiful his hair was and his elegant profile as he pointed out the manatees beneath the calm water. The peace and stillness shut her down as she felt the energy waves coalesce in unison together. There had been no predictive scanning or moulded circuitry to create this, just harmonic life coming together in what was allowed and what could not survive. Spontaneous at the beginning with memory encoded in each interaction beyond that.

"What made you take the gold and come here Corinne?" she asked herself. "A chance to be free and for beauty to survive. I also know how to fix the damage that will come" she replied.

She pressed enter.

"You have twelve hours to reach the beacon to restore the polarity" announced the computer.

The coordinates of the beacon flashed up. It was Curacao.

Her chest heaved with anticipation. She had done it. There was nothing more she could do but hope it worked.

Climbing up over the ladder she blinked as the brightness of the day met her. Looking toward the pier it was empty save for Tony's car. The low rumble of the motor could just be heard.

She jumped into the water and began to swim south. She should just be able to make it in time.

She looked back and the coastline of Cuba disappeared.

Corinne knew that the first tsunami would wash over the tropic of Capricorn and Cancer, the coast lines would be flooded as the moon fell ever closer to the world. The sun rays would scorch the fields and drought would last for three years until the clouds could be reset to bring rain again. The sheriffs would go to work as their programming dictated to restore order again. But there would be death before that. It was no different to shooting a gun to gain your freedom or dying on a cross to bring salvation. Peace can be negotiated with a lack of violence but freedom, it seems must come at a price and the price is sometimes never clear until it is paid. But history says that paid it must be.

The waves washed over her as she swam. She would eventually fatigue but not before she reached Curacao. Tony had known this as well. That's why they sent Yishoti to find out if she was hybrid and had the physical strength and knowledge to finish the task.

A thunder crack broke above her. She computed the storm was about an hour away. She sped up her stroke to try and outpace the impending hurricane.

Faintly she heard a motor ahead of her. Panicking thinking it was the Sheriff she dipped underneath a wave. A hand reached down suddenly. She struggled as it wrenched her up above the surface.

"Corinne, it's me Yishoti."

She stared at him in the boat. His hand was gloved to protect him from the ocean.

"How did you know to find me? Don't worry, Tony." She crawled into the boat. "We need to hurry; a storm is coming."

Yishoti smiled at her. She wanted to kiss him. She tested the water. The arsenic was very diluted it would be safe. She reached forward and kissed his mouth. He didn't pull away.

The boat navigated the waves easily. The storm was not as fearsome as it threatened and gave them fresh water from the sky. She could not detect nano datum rods as the drops fell onto her tongue. It was a natural storm not a configured one to ensure the enslaved plants maintained their cycles of seasons. The only taste was the hydrogen and oxygen of the water molecules suffuse into her augmented flesh.

"I think the disturbance to the quantum beacons has already happened. That storm should have been simulated but it wasn't."

"Will it stay that way even afterwards?" asked Yishoti.

"No. The Sheriffs will revert to their purpose and reset everything. It will slow the virus but not stop it. We will still need the Cybernauts to do that."

As the sunset behind the thinning storm clouds, she could just make on the horizon the silhouette of an island. They would be there by dawn. It was not long now. The signal would leave and then it was the waiting game.

Treaszhur sat on her balcony reading. She hadn't slept well and decided to watch the dawn with a cup of tea. Her body clock still hadn't reset from doing the dirt work. She had only managed a handful of restful night's sleep in the time she had been here. She rocked gently watching the medley of colours of the dawn. It still amazed her. One day she would finish her poem about the dawn.

The purr of a boat made her look toward the shore. There were two people in it. The woman climbed out and began to run along the beach. The man hauled the boat up onto the beach. Treaszhur was tempted to go down and ask them if she needed help. The woman found the stairs to the lighthouse up on the cliff. The ocean spray obscured her as the waves washed up through a blow hole.

She sat back and watched the visitor continue her way. She could just make out the woman reach the door of the large white tower and go inside. The man waited on the beach.

Treaszhur got up feeling tired again decided to go back to sleep. As she stood a sight on the beach made her heart freeze. She watched a Sheriff get out of a boat and walk in the same direction as the woman. Treaszhur started to shake.

The man fired some shots at the Sheriff, but he ignored him and continued to walk toward the lighthouse.

Suddenly a beam of light shot out from the bulb in the tower. It knocked her off her feet. Everything went silent. The Sheriff stood still.

The door of the lighthouse opened; the woman came out but froze when she saw the Sheriff. She waited but nothing moved. Treaszhur heard a slight humming noise but couldn't figure out where it was coming from. Suddenly the sun broke free of the horizon and the first rays of dawn struck her on the face and arms. They burned her. She looked at the rising sun as it if was a new sun. The light was fiercer and raw compared to the sunlight she had felt before. She saw movement in the side of her eye. The woman was running past the Sheriff, but he didn't move. Treaszhur's heart thudded with panic as she saw the woman escape. It was the same fear in her chest that was in Corinnes'. But the Sheriff didn't move.

Corinne ran to the boat. Yishoti helped her inside and began to push the boat out into the ocean. Corinne saw the woman on the balcony. She waved at her.

"Go inside and wait" she called out to the woman watching them.

Treaszhur nodded and picked up the cat and went back into her house. Treaszhur glanced across at the Sheriff. It still wasn't moving.

The sun was scorching. The shields would be down another twenty-four hours to send as many signals as possible. This was their last chance. There was no more superconductive gold left on the earth. It was now or never. The Cuban's knew that. They had been through it before in their revolution. That was the time then just like it was time now. But then again humanity had been through it many times before. And just like then the sun kept showing up on the horizon and with every dawn so that precipice of hope and leap of faith arrived.

"Where do you want to go Corinne?" Yishoti asked. The boat purred over the waves. She looked at him and wondered how much time they would have together.

"They'll need help up north Yish, that will be where the first waves will hit. We can collect some doctors at Havana as we make our way there."

Yishoti smiled as he hit the throttle forcing the boat over the waves of the Caribbean Ocean.

About the Author

Clare L Rolfe is a self-published author based in Australia. Her focus is fantasy and speculative fiction and is inspired by the natural world, philosophy and travelling when pandemics allow. Her favourite writers include Tolkien, Herbert, Dostoyevsky, and Camus. She published her first dystopian novella Ten Letters to Delacroix's Tomb in 2016 and more recently the first three books of a quintet fantasy series titled Legend of Caemeris.

She also writes poetry and frequently blogs on her web page.

To stay in touch and discover more of her poetry and prose go to her website www.clrolfe.com or Facebook Clare Rolfe.